THE CAPSTONE CONUNDRUM

THE CHRONICLES OF KING'S END
BOOK 1.5

CHARITY TAHMASEB

COLLINS MARK BOOKS

The Capstone Conundrum
Copyright © 2025 by Charity Tahmaseb

Paperback ISBN: 978-1-950042-24-1
Hardcover ISBN: 978-1-950042-25-8

Published by Collins Mark Books
Cover copyright © 2025 by Collins Mark Books
Cover design by Collins Mark Books
Interior artwork copyright © ollallya/Depositphotos
Chapter header copyright @ Art_tori/Depositphotos
Umbrella scene break copyright @ baretsky/Depositphotos
Floral interior copyright @ ollallya/Depositphotos
Enclave images copyright:
Crow: @ lifeonwhite/Depositphotos
Umbrella: @ urfingus/Depositphotos
Shield and scroll: @ adroach/Depositphotos

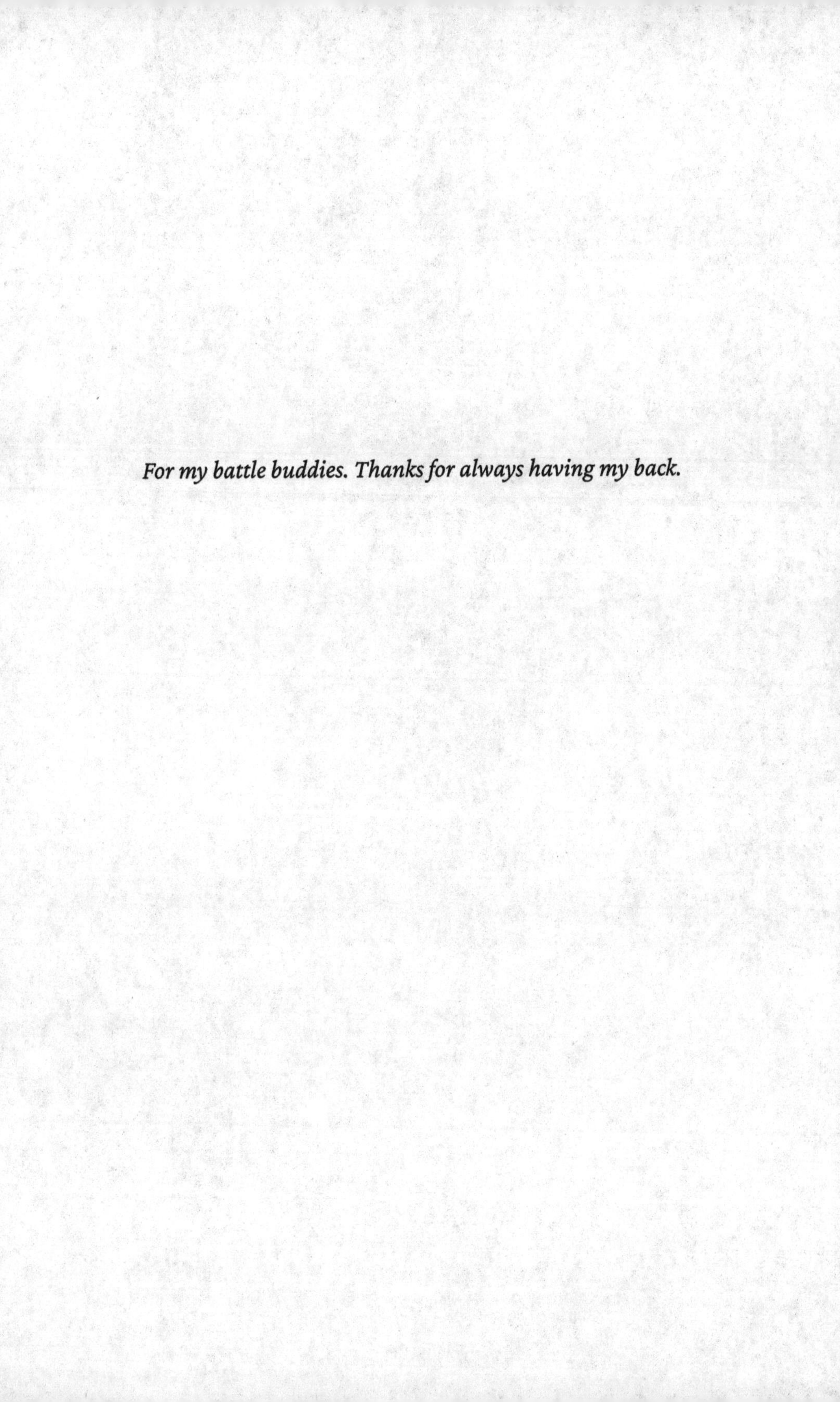

For my battle buddies. Thanks for always having my back.

THE CAPSTONE CONUNDRUM

AUTHOR'S NOTE

The Capstone Conundrum is a companion novella to *The Pansy Paradox*. While technically a prequel, it's meant to be read after the first book in the series. The novella contains spoilers for the series and reveals character and plot developments that will resonate more deeply after reading the novel.

CHAPTER 1
PANSY

Joint Base Lewis-McChord, Washington
Thursday, August 30

No one sleeps the night before graduation. They come for you then. That's the rumor, anyway. Pulling you from the ranks before the sunrise touches Mount Rainier and spiriting you away. No walk of shame in front of your peers. No sitting on the sidelines while others collect accolades and diplomas.

Simply gone.

Bedding stripped, footlocker cleared, closet emptied as if you haven't spent the last twelve weeks in your tiny barracks room with its whitewashed walls, bare floors, and a fluttering sheet for a door.

As if you haven't trained for six grueling summers to protect the world from things most people can't see.

As if you've never wielded an umbrella, held one in your hands, used it to dispatch those things most people can't see.

The night before graduation, no one leaves their umbrella in the stands, the ones at the entrance to each set of barracks. We're supposed to, mind you. Our umbrellas *are* weapons, after all. But not tonight. No one says a word. Even the barracks monitor looks the other way.

She walks the long corridor, fingertips trailing across our barely opaque doors, a gesture meant to reassure us. "It almost never happens," she says, her voice low and soft. "It didn't in my class, at least. You'll be fine. I know you'll all be fine."

We might believe this, too. If not for that caveat.

Almost.

Because it can happen, has happened. We've all heard the stories. Even cadets from the old families get pulled from the ranks for screwing up irrevocably during the capstone exercise. Six years for what? Nothing? I can't imagine it. But I might have to. Because this last week, with our own capstone exercise, *I* may have done the irrevocable.

Worse, I may have brought my two best friends along with me.

Light filters in through the window. It's situated high enough for a modicum of privacy, but—like the floors—it's bare. No curtains for cadets. Lights in the compound shine all night long. In the dim glow, I can trace the fractures in the ceiling. A creak comes from down the hall and above my head. One cadet turning over, bed springs groaning, another testing the floor and heading for the restrooms.

There's no sneaking out tonight. No sticking to the shadows and slinking over to the other barracks, where the cadets destined for field assignments sleep, or not sleep, as the case may be.

But maybe they are sound asleep. Their jobs are more secure than ours, if more competitive. They will go on to see the world while those of us in these barracks will simply go home to our permanent posts.

Next to me, my umbrella flutters her ruffles as if she can soothe me. Over these last twelve weeks, she has given me no end of trouble. She is a flurry of everything I've tried not to be for these last six summers: impulsive, attention-grabbing, effusive.

Now she's nudging me. Since this could be our last night together, I sit up, cradle her in my arms, and ask quietly:

"What's wrong?"

That's when a pebble pings against my window.

My heart rate doubles, a pound, pound, pound that makes my ribs ache. Jack, Mort, and I all agreed we would not do anything so foolish as sneaking out tonight. Too risky, especially with Mort so close to graduating at the top of our class. Yes, he's the sort to take risks, but even he isn't this reckless.

At least, I don't think he is.

Another pebble pings, so I clamber out of bed, grip my umbrella—I'm going nowhere without her tonight—and tiptoe to the window.

Fingertips on the sill, I peer into the night. Below, shrouded in shadows, is not Mort, or Jack. No, instead, grinning up at me, his teeth bright, a flower of undetermined type in his hand, is Charlie Pulchenko. Yes, that's a mouthful, although no more ridiculous than Pansy Little.

I stare in astonishment while my umbrella lets out a long, somewhat exasperated, sigh.

AFTER FIVE MINUTES of hissed exchanges, I relent and let Charlie crawl through my window. He tumbles in with an impressive amount of stealth, it's true. He shakes himself off, unslings his umbrella, and presents me with a somewhat crushed rose.

I've slung my own umbrella cross-body, and now she beats

against my spine. But I take the flower. I even step down the hall and fill a canteen cup with some water in an attempt to revive it. The rose cants to one side. Honestly, it looks fairly despondent, as if it hoped for something more in its final days than whatever this is.

"What are you doing here?" I ask, working to keep my voice low. I sniff and—grateful for the dark—swipe my fingers beneath my nose. As with my umbrella, my Sight has given me no end of trouble this summer as well.

Charlie has taken a seat on my bed. He gives me that blinding grin and pats the space next to him. So, yes, I have a good idea of *what* he wants to do here. Why, though? That makes no sense. Tomorrow is graduation. Chances are we'll never see each other after that.

Then again, maybe that's why he's here.

"It's so boring over there," he says, nodding toward the opposite side of the compound. "Everyone is either drunk or already passed out."

"*What?*" I peer through the window again, toward Charlie's barracks. "What about your barracks monitor?"

"Who do you think bought all the alcohol?"

Are you kidding me? With the parade field illuminated, it's impossible to spy much of anything across the way. Silhouettes flit across windows. A head and shoulders poke through one frame before two hands drag them back inside.

I turn to confront Charlie, arms crossed over my chest, umbrella still vibrating indignantly against my spine. "Seriously? You guys aren't worried?"

"What are they going to do, Pansy? Slap us on the wrist?"

"What if you get caught over here?"

Charlie holds up his hand and gives himself a solid smack on his wrist to demonstrate. "My dad's on the High Council. Do you think the Enclave is going to expel me the night before graduation?"

No, I suppose not. "What about me, then?"

At this, Charlie laughs. He *laughs*.

"You're Rose Little's daughter," he says. "Look. My dad explained it to me, how she got stuck in a permanent post in King's End. But she's still Rose Little, and that has cachet."

Before I attended the Academy, my mother was simply my mother. Fierce? Yes. Able to dispatch Screamers—those invisible things most people can't see—with barely breaking a sweat? Absolutely. But still, my mother. Six summers here have taught me many things about her.

One of those is that she is, according to Enclave lore, legendary. We even studied some of her missions during classroom training. Every time her name popped up, my whole class would swivel to stare at me.

"So, here's the thing." Charlie glances down at his empty hands, and then his gaze travels the room until it lands on the battered, water-stained dresser where the rose droops.

With stealth and agility, he plucks the rose from the canteen. That's one thing about Charlie. Yes, his father sits on the High Council. Yes, he's had all the advantages of growing up in the heart of the Enclave. Strip all that away, and he'll still make a damn good field agent.

He takes a knee in front of me. My umbrella thumps a more strident warning against my spine. Not that I need it. Pressure builds behind my eyes, a combination of the Sight and outright panic. Charlie can't be doing what I think he's doing.

He clears his throat, favors me with a grin, and then intones, voice pitched an octave lower, "Pansy Little, with the permission of my parents, Misha and Anya Pulchenko, I would like to make a formal petition for a betrothal."

Oh, *no*. He is doing what I think he's doing.

Charlie *is* adorable, what with those corkscrew curls, a landscape of freckles across honeyed skin, and that blazing smile. He's been my Academy boyfriend for these past two summers, and after the breakup with Daniel, I'm grateful for that. Charlie's a lot of fun, and I do like him. I also know that in this situation, one of my mother's rules absolutely applies:

When someone tells you they're not betrothed, don't believe them.

Charlie has been betrothed since he was an infant, like most offspring of the old families in the Enclave. Except for me, that is.

"Charlie, what are you doing?"

"Look, my dad can absolutely finesse this. He's already sent the formal request to your mother, along with all the paperwork."

Which she probably tossed in the recycling bin.

"Once we lock that in, he'll petition the High Council. He's got enough backing, and besides, I *really* don't want to marry Leah." Charlie rolls his eyes.

I don't know Leah Connolly, but she was in a few classes ahead of us and has a reputation for being flighty. Jack, with his sense for connections, insists this is a defense mechanism. Leah simply doesn't want to be a field agent, or even part of the Enclave.

Part of me empathizes. Some days, I don't want to, either.

"And she doesn't want to marry me. But!" Here, Charlie springs to his feet and points between the two of us. "*We* like each other, right?"

I nod cautiously.

"And we both need to marry someone in the Enclave, right?"

Technically? No. My mother didn't. Then again, that might be why she's stuck in King's End after all these years. I don't know the reason behind it, but I do know the Enclave won't allow her to leave, not even to attend my graduation ceremony. Assuming, of course, I do graduate.

Charlie barrels forward despite my lack of response.

"So, my dad says that if we do this, you won't have to be a permanent post agent. Don't you want to be in the field?"

He's not wrong. A part of me yearns for that: to be a full-fledged field agent, one sent around the world on assignments. To travel, have adventures, the way my mother did before she became a permanent post agent in King's End. But now that she is, King's End is our territory. It belongs to the Little family, and we're the only two left.

"We could even do field work together!" Charlie continues. "I mean, until the babies come."

Oh, yes. Of course. Have all the freedom and fun you like—*until the babies come.* I try. I mean, I really, really try not to cross my eyes and stick out my tongue at Charlie.

"Why can't *you* stay home with the babies?" I say instead.

Charlie wrinkles his nose as if I've spewed nonsense. "Because after I make principal field agent, I'll take my father's spot on the High Council."

"And I'm going to be a permanent post agent in King's End," I say with more conviction than I feel. That's been my trajectory here at the Academy for the past six years, and there's no changing that the night before graduation.

"You can't be serious."

Here's the thing: I absolutely am. All summer long, the Sight's been humming in the back of my mind, along with a sense of impending doom deep in my belly. Nothing concrete; it hasn't shown me anything. All I have is the sense that I *must* graduate and return to King's End. And while I'm certain to do the latter, I may have screwed up the former.

Before I can explain anything to Charlie, the heavy tread of an unfamiliar set of shoes sounds in the hallway. This is not a cadet. This is certainly not our barracks monitor. Her steps are light, her knowledge of all the creaking floorboards exceptional. She's worked overtime this summer not to disturb what little sleep we get.

These footfalls are purposeful, full of agency and authority.

And they've just halted right outside my room.

CHAPTER 2
PANSY

Joint Base Lewis-McChord, Washington
Friday, August 24 (one week prior)

My umbrella and Jack's are whispering. Their tips touch and, every once in a while, the ruffles on my umbrella flutter. In response, the silver threads in Jack's seem to glow. Like us, they are best friends.

The Enclave insists this sort of thing doesn't happen. Our umbrellas aren't sentient; they are simply so finely tuned that they pick up on our emotions, the churning in our subconscious, and elements of what Freud might call the id. Our umbrellas are mere extensions of ourselves and nothing more—a utilitarian tool that can be used for offense or defense. For some cadets, that seems to be the case. Their umbrellas have all the animation of the store-bought variety.

Then there's mine.

She has a mind and a will of her own. So does Jack's, although his is considerably calmer, a slate gray with flashes of silver. My umbrella? What a frivolous thing. Pink, with white polka dots of all sizes. And ruffles. So many ruffles.

I'm supposed to keep a low profile during my training, not call attention to myself. This is the one iron-clad rule my mother has set down for me. The Enclave can't know I have the Sight, or rather, how strong it is. So far, I've managed that, disguising what I can't hide with the catch-all excuse of mild premonitions. That's common enough, and the cadre routinely dismisses those. In the process, they've also dismissed me.

But traipsing around with something that resembles a Victorian maiden's parasol is not helping matters.

Thankfully, at the moment, Jack's umbrella is keeping mine occupied. Our class has assembled in a clearing, already split into two teams, waiting for the capstone exercise briefing. The capstone exercise is our final test. It will determine class ranking, assignments for those heading for the field, and whether those of us heading home will be allowed to keep our umbrellas.

The sky is a deep blue above us, bordered by evergreens. The scent of pine lingers in the air. Occasionally, a hint of salt flavors the breeze, but really, we're too far away from Puget Sound for that.

The earth is rough and damp beneath us. Yes, we're all sitting on the ground. No chairs for cadets. We haven't seen our barracks in two weeks, and we all stink like it. Still, it's a communal stench. The only people who notice are the evaluators.

Much to our delight.

Mort has even made it his mission to reek as much as possible, as if the stench will help him graduate at the top of our class. And he really does stink, a funk that announces his presence before his boots or voice can. I'm glad he's standing up front, as our team lead, in a row that includes the cadre and evaluators.

He's waiting, they're waiting, we're all waiting, an endless stretch of time that's making our legs numb. It's as if the Enclave has adopted the military's motto of *hurry up and wait*. Since we're somewhere on Joint Base Lewis-McChord, it makes a certain amount of sense. Although I doubt the military has ever waited on Professor Reginald Botten.

Then again, maybe they have.

This pause flavors the air as well. Instead of a much-needed break, everyone is on edge. Instead of a respite, it's like trying to quench our thirst with seawater. This delay feels deliberate. Because beneath it lingers an undercurrent of malice.

I glance at Jack, and he nods. No doubt he feels it, too.

At last, the tires of a Humvee crunch over a barely-there dirt road. The vehicle churns up dust and exhaust. When Professor Botten steps from the passenger side, in full field gear, I drop my gaze to my knees.

The Sight is insisting I must roll my eyes. I don't have time to lock it down. The single thought blazes through my mind, cuts through all my defenses. Why, I don't know. It's nothing but dangerous. The Sight—in its own way—is all about self-preservation, and Professor Botten has an instinct for insolence. An eyeroll? *Major* insolence. A week ago, he dressed down Charlie for one, in front of our entire class, the cadre, and the evaluators.

While my mother never mentioned Professor Botten by name, I know that his attention may not just end my hopes of graduating, but—somehow—end *me*.

It's a nonsensical sort of thought. The Enclave wants us to graduate; they need agents in the field and at permanent posts. Yes, competition is high for those destined for field assignments. Yes, they'll weed out the inadequate. I've been working to go unnoticed, and when I am noticed, to be unremarkable. Not so much to put my post in King's End in jeopardy, but enough to remain off the cadre's radar and Professor Botten's in particular.

Why I sense a strange wave of loathing whenever his attention strays my way, I can't say.

Jack passes me an olive drab handkerchief before I can tug out my own. He shifts and blocks the cadre's view. I catch the blood dripping from my nose, the Sight's annoying physical tell, and then clutch the handkerchief in my fist, just in case. Over the past six years, he's become adept at this sort of thing: a handkerchief, a deflection, a distraction.

"You okay?" he asks.

"Yeah. Just"—I give my head a quick shake—"one of those things."

Jack's gaze flits from Professor Botten and then back to me, a frown gathering on his brow. He gives his own head a shake, as if he can't make sense of what he's detecting. Then, suddenly, he blurts a single word.

"Rose."

A few cadets sitting near us shoot him warning glances. Someone presses a finger to their lips and nods toward the front. No one is addressing us yet. It's a bunch of glad-handing and congratulations aimed at the team leads. Mort is eating it up, a cocky swell to his chest. I want to warn him not to get overconfident. That, as the Sight knows, will not end well.

"What?" I whisper to Jack.

"It's not you." He tilts his head toward the front, in Botten's direction. "It's your mom. It's—I can't really describe it, but yeah, he has ... feelings, lots of them. It's like your mom is living rent-free in his head."

That's weird. "She's never mentioned him. It's almost like he doesn't exist."

Jack huffs a breath of quiet laughter. "Yeah. That fits." He sobers and gives my hand a squeeze. "We'll just keep you away from him. It's not like he's personally conducting the evaluations."

True, but as headmaster of the Academy, he certainly approves every last one.

"It'll be fine," Jack says. "I know it will. We're all making it through this. You, me, Mort. It's a lock."

Part of me wants to believe him. His sense for connections runs strong, but bias can distort them. And when it comes to me, Jack is most definitely biased.

Professor Botten steps forward. His smile is benevolent, but not all-encompassing, reserved for those on the Botten's Best List. Most cadets work overtime to be on that list. Botten is someone you'd want on your side and wouldn't want as an enemy. Nearly everyone tries to curry his favor and make the cut for the list.

In addition to being headmaster of the Academy, he sits on the Enclave's High Council, where, as rumor has it, he doles out the plum assignments. The only way to get one of those, again, as rumor has it, is to kiss some serious ass. Long after graduation, Botten can make or break your career in the Enclave.

This is one thing I won't have to worry about as a permanent post agent in King's End.

Professor Botten clears his throat then, and the last whispers among the cadets fade. His low, sonorous voice rings out across the clearing.

While I know it's nonsensical, once again, something in his tone tells me he could—and absolutely might—break me.

CHAPTER 3
JACK

Joint Base Lewis-McChord, Washington
Friday, August 24

Jack Ling is anxious, and being anxious is one of his least favorite things. His mentor, his Uncle George, mentioned that the feeling would assault him this summer, crawl up his spine, wrap fingers around his throat and squeeze.

His uncle has a similar sense for connections, can read those strange, invisible threads that tie one person to another, or to a particular place. Some threads are strong; others are weak. Discerning which are which?

That, according to his uncle, is an undertaking of a lifetime.

But this last summer at the Academy means that many of those threads will snap. Relationships will end, friendships disintegrate. Someone in their class will not walk at graduation. Jack can't confess this to Pansy, because he doesn't know who that person is. No one feels safe. Not even Mort, who should graduate with top honors. The capstone exercise is his to lose.

Except, as Jack knows all too well, Mort has never met a risk he didn't want to take. He will risk everything and everyone during this coming week, and that includes Pansy.

The canopy of his umbrella ripples in commiseration, and the ruffles on Pansy's flutter as if to assure him that no matter what happens, the three of them will be okay.

But Jack isn't so sure. Since they became a trio their second summer, Mort has used Pansy—or rather, her Sight—relentlessly, something that makes Jack's stomach churn and has him staring at the barracks ceiling late into the night.

That something casts a dark shroud on the capstone briefing. Not that they need to listen, not really. No one's giving away clues, Professor Botten in particular, not even when he says:

"As is our tradition, the capstone is based on an actual field mission. Let's see if you can outsmart your parents' generation."

A cheer goes up in response. Professor Botten continues, intoning about the Enclave's sacred and secret duty to protect this dimension from those things that disrupt it—those things being Screamers. They're not supposed to call them that, although everyone does, even the cadre. One, Screamers *do* scream in the moment they attack. Two, shouting, "Watch out for those temporal disturbances!" is ridiculous.

Professor Botten launches into the formal portion of the mission brief, and Jack tunes out almost immediately. He suspects the details—hints of ancient roads, rolling hills, domes and spires, and something that tastes like salt from the Ligurian Sea—are seeding misinformation. The less he takes in, the better. At the moment, though? He would gladly trade the damp Pacific Northwest for sun-soaked Italy.

Those in the front rows—butt-kissers, every last one—are staring raptly or furiously scribbling notes. For all the good it will do them. Why must there be a layer of duplicity to everything the Enclave does?

This, too, is something his uncle has warned him about. Not everyone is deceitful. In fact, the strongest deceit can flow from those who lie, not to others, but to themselves. When Jack pressed, insisted on knowing about the headmaster of the Academy, his uncle was strangely evasive.

"Go with your instincts there," was all his mentor said.

But Jack doesn't know which of those to trust.

Keeping Pansy away from Botten and helping Mort win the capstone? That *feels* right, and Jack has made it his mission. With the briefing winding down and the teams spreading out across the clearing, that mission starts now.

Mort strides across the trampled grass and draws both Jack and Pansy into a huddle. She winces and wrinkles her nose. Jack pretends to cough like he's choking on exhaust from Botten's Humvee.

"Very funny," Mort says. "Enough. Tell me what you think." He nods toward the cluster of cadre and evaluators, also in a huddle.

"I was barely listening," Jack says.

"I wasn't listening at all," Pansy adds.

Mort surveys both of them, arms crossed over his chest. "Okay. Tell me what you *feel*."

Jack shuts his eyes, breathes in not only Mort's stench but the compound at large. The wave of competing emotions is almost too much. They batter against his mind, a hurricane wind against storm shutters. He wonders how Pansy is handling it, although she can lock down her Sight and function as if none of this chaos is clogging the air.

At last, he opens his eyes and confronts the startling blue of Mort's. It was Mort's eyes that first drew Jack in, and it's those eyes that keep him coming back, keep him trusting that—someday—Mort will be the person Jack perceives in their depths.

"Keep it clean," Jack says.

"Really?" Mort gives his head a shake. "But I have a whole squad—"

"No."

"But Botten—"

"*No.*"

"Shit."

"They're going to deduct points for that," Pansy chimes in, and then presses the handkerchief to her nose.

"Actually deduct?" Mort glances around the clearing, his gaze straying toward the other team, led by Charlie Pulchenko. *That has caused more than its share of conflict, even when Jack assures Mort that Pansy is not serious about Charlie and wouldn't betray them like that.*

"Would you really sabotage other members of the Enclave—" Jack begins.

"Oh, absolutely."

"—in the field?"

No, not in the field. Anywhere else? Of course. What was it Rose always said? That Enclave headquarters is steeped in ambition, avarice, and malice. The field is different. There, everything is stripped away. No matter how much you loathe the agents next to you, you need them, and they need you. Depending on the crisis, you either all work together, or you all die.

"Then, why not mention that?" Mort asks.

"They want us to be smart enough to figure it out," Jack says.

Mort rubs his face and then pushes his hands through his dirty blond hair, which is greasier and darker than usual. All three of them look the worse for wear. Jack peers at the world through smudged lenses. While he's wearing a clean pair of socks, he can't remember when he last brushed his teeth. Pansy has disguised bloodstains with smears of mud on her field shirt. She looks as if she low-crawled her way from their command post.

"You'd think they'd train us without all these mind games." Mort considers the team across the way, where Charlie's in a similar huddle with his own intel analyst. "You know he's going to—"

"You planned on deploying security, right?"

"Of course."

Jack shrugs. "Well, there you go."

Frustration rolls off Mort. He's a little too good at sabotaging the other team—and sabotage in general. That's not a skill you need in the field. Although, for climbing the Enclave's career ladder? Even Jack has to admit it could come in handy.

"You two are both sure?"

He and Pansy nod.

"All right." Mort heaves a sigh. "We'll keep it clean."

CHAPTER 4
PANSY

Joint Base Lewis-McChord, Washington
Friday, August 24

Mort is frantic and angry and trying to keep it clean. His swearing has gone from creative to crude and has Jack rolling his eyes. Our squads have all been hit because Charlie is not keeping it clean, not that anyone's surprised. After each strike, Mort casts me a withering look, as if I'm somehow responsible for how Charlie runs his team.

"Traitor," Mort mutters, but despite the rancor in his voice, I know he doesn't mean it.

The squad leaders want to hit back. Their frustration floods our tiny command post, congesting the air as much as exhaust from all those Humvees. Then again, that might simply be the lack of showers. Mort silences them not only with another withering glance, but a proclamation as well.

"Would you waste resources like that on a real field mission?"

Everyone shakes their heads. Because no, you wouldn't. You'd deploy a single squad to perform security to keep the locals away from the target area. Nothing like having Screamers chase you onto private property only to find yourself staring up at the barrel of a twelve-gauge shotgun. Or explaining to law enforcement why you're performing intricate acrobatics in an abandoned field.

With an umbrella.

Normally, the cadre roleplay locals and law enforcement. However, over the last five summers, they've tacitly encouraged us to do the same and hinder the other team's ability to complete their mission.

Mort says they're lazy. The more we hit the other team, the less the cadre have to. Jack insists they're bored. There are only so many times you can pretend to be Farmer Brown or Sheriff Smith. We never earn points for any of these hits. But we certainly lose points, especially if we can't deal with local interference, no matter how unrealistic those scenarios might be or who is providing the interference.

This is why Mort has switched me from pinpointing fissures to predicting the next attack. I'm good at locating fissures, both real ones and the simulated ones the cadre create for the capstone exercise. One of those fissures conceals a fake level five hot spot. This is the goal of the capstone exercise: find that fissure, locate, then neutralize, the level five hot spot and lock it down.

Mort really needs me on fissure duty, but he can't bear the idea of Charlie making him look bad, of taking hits without striking back. It goes against everything Mort is: brave, bold, and brash. Charlie is waging a war of attrition in hopes that it will be the deciding factor as it has been for all the exercises before this one.

After Mort sends the squads out again, he comes to stand behind us and stares at the map. "We're never going to win if we're constantly playing defense."

He's right, in a sense. Charlie's team is eating away at our score. In addition to the level five hot spot, points are tallied by the number of fissures we discover and repair, the ambushes we anticipate, and the Screamers—some real, some virtual—we dispatch.

Here in the tent, we're safe. The olive drab canvas is reinforced with the fabric used in the canopies of our umbrellas, the supports similar to the poles and ribs. These two things, working together, create a protective bubble. Screamers can't touch us, at least not inside the tent.

The moment we step outside? All bets are off.

It's safe enough inside the tent that I can shut my eyes and let both my index fingers travel the map. Yes, we use an actual paper map, one that's laminated. Because electronics can fail, we need to know how to do this job without assistance. My fingertips halt, almost of their own volition. My head is down, so the drops of blood land on the ground and not on my somewhat disgusting field shirt.

Jack swoops in and sticks a pin in both locations and then slips me a fresh handkerchief. I think they're Army surplus. In any case, he has an unending supply.

Mort anchors me with a solid hand to my shoulder. "What do you see, Pansy?"

I taste more than see, sense more than know. None of this is exact. It might not even be true, never mind accurate. This is how the Sight works. It's precarious, perverse, and totally unpredictable. But these glimpses are so close, so real—I can see a gravel crossroads and then, elsewhere, a pine-laced ravine. Certainty simmers in my chest, and I can't help but smile.

"Here." I point to the first pin, the crossroads where we have an outpost set up. "Charlie is planning a major hit on us right here."

"Major?" Mort asks.

"Two squads, at least." I consider the canvas above my head, touch the Sight again and let it go. I know Charlie and the games he likes to play. While reaching for the details is risky, something tells me we absolutely need them. "Law enforcement, possible arrests if we can't talk our way out of it. Some cadre will be there, too."

Mort swears. "How am I supposed to—"

"But here," I say, my finger traveling across the terrain to the other pin. "This, right here? That's the level five hot spot."

Mort grasps both shoulders now and turns me to stare down into my face. "You're sure."

"As much as I can be. I can try—"

"No." Jack's voice is taut. "Don't push her, Mort. She's got that look. And she can't"—he glances around the command post, at the few others gathered here—"not in front of everyone."

No, I really can't afford to succumb to an all-out attack of the Sight, not during the capstone, not in front of anyone other than Jack and Mort. But the hot spot. There's only one. The team that finds it first earns major points, not enough to win, but more than enough to counteract all those hits Charlie's been flinging our way.

Mort steps back. Then he crouches, hands on his head, but no one steps near him. This, as we all know, is his thinking posture. He fairly radiates with the effort, as does his umbrella, a blue blur slung cross-body. It's like he's gathering all his thoughts and all his considerable strength.

Then he pops to his feet. "Keep verifying what you can," he says to us before turning toward the operations specialists.

"Sandeep, Carmen, I've got an idea. Let's huddle."

"Hey, buddy." Mort claps Jack on the shoulder. "I've got a proposition for you."

"Now's hardly the time," I mutter.

Jack snorts. Mort jabs a finger in my direction but keeps talking as if I haven't said a thing.

"If Charlie's so intent on hitting us, I'm thinking let him. We'll keep a squad at the outpost. If we lose them, then we lose them. But I'm taking everyone else to find the hot spot. You and Pansy will stay here."

"Alone?"

"Unless you think the attack is a ruse. Charlie's not going to hit our command post instead, is he?"

Jack is shaking his head, and without thinking, I do the same. Alone, though? Just the two of us? I'm not sure I like this.

"We need to keep someone here," Mort says. "You know that."

We can't leave the command post unattended. In a practical sense, someone needs to collect all the data being relayed from the squads, and someone needs to send intelligence back out again. Besides all that, if one of the evaluators finds the command post unattended? That's a major point deduction, one worse than all the hits we've been taking.

"Can't someone from operations stay, maybe Sandeep or—?"

"You got this." Mort gives Jack's shoulder a squeeze. "You're more than an intel analyst, okay? I trust you to do the right thing."

Jack nods, his expression stoic, but doubt floats heavily in the air. I take his hand and give it a squeeze as well.

Mort moves toward the tent flaps. Before he steps through, he adds, "I don't care about Charlie, but send any updates you get about the hot spot." While this is directed at both of us, beneath the innocuous command is another—less obvious one—for me.

Mort wants me to use the Sight as much as I dare, to touch the corners of it, maybe even go a little deeper, have Jack anchor me to the present and wade in. Not too far, maybe up to my knees, figuratively speaking. With everyone gone, it's a risk worth taking.

Still, the command post is strangely silent, hushed in a way that feels wrong. Like an empty school or deserted gymnasium. Usually, an industrious hum fills this space. We're stepping over and reaching around each other, calling out updates for the operations team to relay to those in the field.

Now, everything is so quiet. If not for unease churning low in my belly, I'd enjoy the birdsong and the whisper of the breeze through the pines.

"I don't like this, Pansy."

Jack's expression and voice are so forlorn. I don't know what he's sensing, and I'm not even sure he could articulate it if he tried.

"Charlie's not going to hit us," I say, trying to bolster him.

It works, sort of. Jack even laughs. "Yeah, I *know* that. And Charlie knows that if he does, you won't speak to him again, never mind anything else. He wants to win, but he's not that stupid."

Well … yes. Not that this warning is something I've put into so many words with Charlie. It's one thing to try to sabotage Mort, but Charlie knows I'm always in a support role, always in the command post and never on patrol.

Which is fine, since I'll be doing plenty of my own patrolling when I return to King's End.

I step toward the map and consider Mort's unspoken request.

"Pansy—" Jack's voice is low, even though it's only us here.

"I'm okay."

"Look, I'm not stupid, either. I know what Mort wants you to do." He glances around the tent. "I think that's why he left us alone. But I don't think you should. Even if it means losing, I don't think you should."

Well, I never *should*. To be fair, it often isn't even my fault. The

Sight simply attacks; that's what it feels like, at least. It has an agenda of its own. Over the years, I've learned to lock it down and sidestep its insistence. Even so? I can't always escape it. If I could predict when it's going to give me a bloody nose or when it plans to knock me sideways, my life would be a whole lot easier.

I reach a hand behind me, and Jack takes it. This is the capstone. It's worth the risk.

"Five minutes," he says. "No more. I'm timing it."

The first wave washes over me. I barely hear him, his voice more of an echo. Something's been bothering me about the hot spot, something crucial, a nonstop nattering in the back of my mind. Not the location. That's correct. If Mort is quick, he'll find it first. Charlie, the Sight insists, doesn't have a clue. The only way his team will find the hot spot is if they stumble across it. Granted, Charlie has that sort of luck, but Mort is faster.

But something is definitely wrong with the hotspot itself. What's curious is that the Sight doesn't seem to be showing me the here and now in the Pacific Northwest, although I can see endless trees and inhale crisp, clean air. I turn, searching this vision, but omnipresent Mount Rainier is nowhere. It doesn't confirm any of Botten's, clues either. I suspect Italy is a lie.

A second wave strikes me, stronger this time. I waver, grip Jack's hand, but his fingers slip through my mine. I'm crashing, crashing hard, in a way I haven't for months. My world goes red— a sailor's warning of a color—before everything dims to a single pinpoint of light. Then that, too, winks out.

The last thing I sense is Jack catching me before I hit the ground.

CHAPTER 5
JACK

Panic and anger and resentment pump through Jack's veins in time with his pulse, which has skyrocketed. Damn Mort, anyway. Jack *knew*. Of course he did. He always does. Pansy had that look: the Sight was hovering, just waiting to strike.

At least they're alone. At least he can clean up the blood, and make her as comfortable as possible by fashioning his field jacket into a makeshift pillow. Now, the next question. Let her sleep it off? Or try to bring her back?

No one would nap during the capstone exercise. If any of the squads return? There are so few of their teammates he can trust to keep Pansy's secret. Sandeep, maybe. In fact, Jack's fairly certain Sandeep already suspects.

Still, it's better if no one knows for certain.

Jack kneels next to Pansy. The Sight always leaves her startlingly still, like Snow White in her glass coffin. A fairy tale princess living under a curse. Except Pansy is far too fierce for that. He knows she'll fight her way back eventually. Maybe he can help.

With precision and care, he lets his fingers come to rest at her temples. Rose helped him refine this technique well beyond what the Academy teaches, as if she'd anticipated this very thing. The strength of this attack nearly has him jerking his hands away. It's been building all summer. The residue left in the Sight's wake is thick and sticky and vast.

Jack knows he can relieve some of that burden and give Pansy a fighting chance to surface, and to do so quickly.

That's when he hears the snap of twigs, the crunch of boots, and the steady approach of more than one person.

Shit. What he needs is Mort watching his back. Jack can't do this alone, not if he needs to remain on guard as well. He stands, peers out the tent flaps. Maybe it's simply a patrol returning. He'll send them right back out again. Problem solved, right?

Then a low, sonorous voice joins the crackle of footfalls on underbrush. It's a sound to freeze his soul. A second voice, this one pitched louder. Deliberately? As a courtesy? Or an early warning? Jack thinks so. He'd be grateful, too, if not for the fact that Pansy is still unconscious and the two people heading for the command post are Professor Botten and Principal Field Agent Henry Darnelle.

There's no hiding the Sight from either of them.

His umbrella vibrates with a frantic alert. Jack has less than a minute before the two men push their way through the tent flaps, discover Pansy and all the blood. He starts there, kicking dirt over the obvious spots, dumping out his canteen on some others, then leaving it there, on its side, cap unscrewed.

It's not great camouflage, but it's better than nothing.

He slings Pansy's umbrella over his shoulder. The panicky

beat of both canopies against his spine urges him on. He surveys the command post. They'll lose points for this, maybe enough to forfeit the exercise, with top honors going to Charlie Pulchenko rather than Mort.

The other outcome? The Enclave discovering Pansy's Sight? Rose's voice plays in his head, those soft, almost desperate words she spoke the year both he and Mort visited for Thanksgiving. The plaintive appeal she made while the two of them prepared dinner together, alone in the kitchen.

This is a request I hate to make, Jack, dear. It's so unfair. But whatever you do, please help Pansy keep her Sight hidden. Her life may depend on it.

This, Jack has always intuited, from the first weeks during their first summer together. Pansy's Sight is extraordinary. That the evaluators haven't picked up on it astounds him. But Pansy is so very good at hiding it. Rose never mentioned what the Enclave might do if they discovered it, but Jack could taste her fear. They'd rip Pansy away, use her, maybe to the point where she'd end up in a Sight-induced coma for the rest of her life.

Maybe Rose Little never mentioned Professor Reginald Botten, either. Maybe he doesn't live rent-free in her head the way she does in his. Maybe it's Jack's imagination and fear fueling his thoughts. But he knows this: The danger comes not just from the Enclave, but the man pushing his way through the evergreens on his way to their command post.

Jack spares a precious moment to secure the tent flaps for both doors, knotting them tight. Then he shimmies beneath the far wall of the tent and tugs Pansy out as gently as possible. He's not as strong as Mort, but he's carried Pansy before. The canopies of both umbrellas flutter as if that might give him strength.

He heaves her up as best he can and plunges into the woods,

down treacherous paths and then veering deeper into the pines, breaking his own trail.

Branches claw at his face, roots reach up and grab at his legs until, at last, one triumphs. Jack's ankle crumples beneath him. He grips Pansy tight so when she rolls from his arms, it's mere inches rather than feet from the ground.

He pants, tests his ankle, and collapses again. He braces his hands on the ground, swallows back pain that radiates up his leg, through his chest, and all the way to his throat. Then Jack crawls to where Pansy is, oddly serene, as if they hadn't just crashed and burned.

With effort, his ankle singing out with every move, he tugs her into a depression behind a large, lone oak. He unfurls both umbrellas and positions them so they create a protective bubble. He's not worried about the virtual Screamers, not this deep in the woods. The cadre don't like to get their hands—or field uniforms—that dirty.

But real ones? That could be a problem.

He's not worried about Botten. The professor won't venture this far into the woods, either.

But Henry Darnelle? That could be another problem, one more dangerous than mere Screamers.

Jack rests his back against the oak, Pansy's head on his thigh and his fingertips on her temples. The Sight still clings to her mind. The sensation of that almost obliterates the agony in his ankle.

And now? All Jack can do is stare up into the oak's branches and the sky beyond.

All he can do is wait.

CHAPTER 6
HENRY

Joint Base Lewis-McChord, Washington
Friday, August 24

Newly appointed Principal Field Agent Henry Darnelle was annoyed. The man at his side? Professor Reginald Botten? The main source of that annoyance.

Still, watching Botten plow into the tent door rather than through it? Amusing. To the point that Henry's lips twitched. As was the fact that some enterprising cadet had knotted the ties beyond untangling.

Less amusing? Botten expected Henry to unravel the situation, which he did by carefully plucking at the ties rather than slicing through them, much to Botten's own annoyance.

The command post was—unsurprisingly—empty when they stepped inside.

"Not like Cadet Connolly to leave his command center unattended." Botten gestured to the tablet Henry held. "Automatic deduction."

Had Henry been alone, he'd give the poor cadet left in charge the benefit of the doubt. They'd probably stepped out to relieve themselves and had no plans for returning until after both he and Botten had left. Not that Henry blamed them.

He logged the necessary deduction and cringed. Damn Botten for dragging him into this, anyway. But every field agent needed to "give back" in some capacity. Research sabbaticals were a popular choice, and so very tempting. But two years away from the field? Two years when his skills might languish and grow rusty? No. He'd opted for the shorter, if more annoying, capstone evaluator role.

Besides, he'd be working with many of these cadets once they'd graduated. The capstone exercise was a construct, true. Still, it gave him a good sense for strengths and weaknesses. Plus, a month in Seattle? That gave him time with his family, his father in particular.

Worry tinged his thoughts. Something was off there, with his father, and only recently so. Henry needed to investigate that, but before he could think further, his umbrella gave him the slightest nudge.

Botten had been nattering on and then abruptly stopped. Henry pulled his attention back to the man who, after all, held his next assignment in his hands.

"Interesting," the professor said. He pointed to the map. "Looks like they uncovered the hot spot."

"Impressive." For only hours into the exercise, it was. Henry tilted the tablet away from Botten and surreptitiously added a few points to the tally. True, Mortimer Connolly was a loose cannon, but there was no denying his ability to take the right sort of risks. It was an innate skill, and one the Academy simply couldn't teach.

"Perhaps. And perhaps not." Botten toed the dark, damp earth beneath the map. "Granted, Cadet Connolly was impressive that first summer. I had my eye on him even then, but he was exceptionally so starting with the second. I suspect there's more than one reason for that."

"And that would be?"

With the tip of his umbrella, Botten speared a discarded handkerchief, one fairly drenched with blood. The image burst bright in Henry's mind. All that blood meant one thing, and one thing only.

"I didn't realize this class had someone with the Sight." Henry scrolled through the list of cadets, but none of them was earmarked with anything more than mild premonitions or a sense for connections. Still. "Cadet Ling, perhaps?"

Botten shook his head. "No, he's been thoroughly tested. He'll make an exceptional intelligence analyst, make no mistake. In fact, I look forward to having him at headquarters. But he doesn't possess the Sight." He cast Henry a sly look. "You know what that looks like."

Indeed, Henry did. He'd been yanked from the field during Ophelia's capstone exercise, where she'd indulged her Sight to the point that no one on staff could rouse her. It'd been left to Henry, and it had taken him the better part of the day and into the night.

Ophelia's first question when she did emerge?

"How much did we win by?"

Henry covered his mouth to hold in the sigh. His reckless, reckless little sister.

"Someone may have cut themselves," he ventured, even though he could read this sort of blood splatter. The mess the Sight left in its aftermath was distinctive, startling, and always sent a rush of anxiety through his veins.

Botten cast him another *you know better* look. Yes, Henry did.

"All right, then," he said. "Any idea who it might be?"

"None. I've pressed Cadet Connolly. He knows things before

he should." With the tip of his umbrella, Botten tapped the location of the hot spot, leaving behind a splotch of blood-soaked mud. "Obviously. But he simply gives me that blank Connolly stare and shrugs."

Oh, yes, the Connollys were experts at feigning innocence; it was always a bad idea to assume they were. Ophelia, technically a Connolly herself, could project an air of naiveté so astounding that you had no choice but to believe her. Between that and the Sight, she'd evaded so many punishments growing up—or had left him to take the blame.

"I was hoping that your familiarity with the Sight might lead you to discover who this might be," Botten said now.

Speaking of Ophelia. There it was: the real reason Henry was tagged this year, for this particular class. Not to evaluate, but to expose someone's secret.

"We've narrowed the field," Botten continued, "to someone on Cadet Connolly's team, most likely chosen repeatedly. You could dig through the records, see which names pop up, time and time again, starting with that second year."

Certainly, someone had already done *that* and had come up empty. Henry went with a noncommittal, "Hm."

"You don't approve?"

This was a narrow line to walk. If Henry were completely honest with himself, he'd admit that he didn't approve, not entirely. Something about this whole enterprise with Botten felt off. Ophelia, with her Sight, could probably tell him why.

Instead of answering, Henry crouched and examined the egress route under the tent wall. Two cadets, he was fairly certain. Was one incapacitated? He rubbed his fingers across his eyes, sore from lack of sleep, gritty from time in the field. Oh, he dearly hoped not.

"Think of it, my boy. Another agent in the Enclave, with an

ability to rival your sister's?" Botten ran the tip of his umbrella across the map from pinpoint to pinpoint, the location of each fissure precise. "That might take some pressure off Ophelia."

Rival. Interesting word, that. Henry could imagine any number of scenarios where Ophelia and another agent might be pitted against each other, pushed to the breaking point. Ophelia, at least, had the protection of her father, Arthur Connolly, chair of the High Council. This other person? Henry studied the evidence of that mad dash beneath the tent wall. They might not have those sorts of privileges.

"Let's take a look around outside," Botten suggested, his tone bored and tinged with disappointment.

They stepped from the tent—after Henry had unknotted the ties to the back door—and surveyed the surrounding area. The woods were thick, full of unforgiving branches, rotting logs, and enough growth that no one could approach the command post without making a racket. Clever, that. Henry added an extra few points to Team Connolly's score.

There were also plenty of places to hide. He wasn't about to wade in and start beating the bushes with his umbrella, although Botten looked on the verge of insisting he do just that.

A shudder raced down his spine, surprising and disconcerting, and wholly from his umbrella. Henry turned his back to the woods. So unlike his umbrella to act up. It had been in stealth mode for most of the exercise so far, its boredom hardly feigned. But now it was clearly agitated about something.

Or perhaps it was merely his own agitation. What good would it do to expose a sixth-year cadet? This shielding—or whatever it was—was intentional. Everyone in the Enclave monitored their children for the Sight. The Academy ran brutal tests to force latent skills to the surface.

And Botten's interest? That had always left Henry feeling

uneasy. The man's obsession went beyond the practical. If Henry had to give it a name, he'd call it prurient. That unease only grew when Botten had turned his gaze toward Ophelia and her extraordinary ability. As celebrated as Ophelia and her Sight were, danger always lurked—be it incapacitation, or even a coma. Some families wanted to spare their children all that.

So, when his umbrella nudged him again? Henry stepped to the left, letting his boot cover the telltale trail of blood leading into the woods. Whoever this cadet was, they deserved both privacy and the privilege of making their own decision.

Still, it wasn't so much the Sight that impressed him, but this cadet's ability to hide it. For six long summers! Now, *that* was extraordinary. What he wouldn't give to speak with this particular cadet, learn how they controlled the Sight, perhaps uncover techniques that might help Ophelia not be at the mercy of her own.

Henry cast a final look at the woods before leading Botten away.

Somewhere in the lush vegetation, there were answers. So be it. Henry supposed he was destined never to find out.

CHAPTER 7
JACK

Joint Base Lewis-McChord, Washington
Friday, August 24

Jack smells Mort's anger—along with Mort—long before he crashes down the hillside and through the camouflage Jack set up earlier. The shelter explodes in a flurry of pine needles, umbrellas canting to the side, the protective bubble fracturing.

"You. Have. Ruined. Everything." Mort's cheeks are flushed an aggressive pink, the color deepening toward heart-attack red. "What the hell is going on? Why did you leave the command post?" He continues the tirade, lacing every other sentence with a stream of obscenities so foul, they should wilt the surrounding underbrush.

Jack swallows against the tightness in his throat. He lets Mort berate him. Because, yes, Jack has screwed up royally and ruined everything: Mort's chances at graduating with top honors, the capstone exercise, Jack's own class ranking. A thought spikes through Jack's mind. Maybe *he's* the cadet who won't walk at graduation.

"You should've seen Darnelle. The last thing I need is his effing pity. It was all over his face. He knows we've lost." Mort hunches over as if the pain of that is too much to bear.

No, Jack didn't see Principal Field Agent Henry Darnelle, but he heard him, Professor Botten, and the conversation that echoed on the ridge far above. Jack spent the last half an hour soaked in sweat, not daring to take a full breath, never mind shifting his position, even when his ankle throbbed.

He even pulled his hands from Pansy's temples, the sensation of her Sight practically burning his fingertips. Whether that was his own instinct or the Sight's self-preservation mode, he couldn't tell. But she remained silent and alarmingly still. With both Botten and Agent Darnelle lingering on the ridge above them, that seemed for the best.

Until Botten's ostensibly benign proclamation: "I am disappointed, Cadet Connolly. I expected better from you."

The cold silence that follows those words, the condemnation in each footfall, tears—scorching and sour—that Mort held back. Jack could taste it all.

"You couldn't stay in the command post," Mort continues, his breath hot and his words bitter. "You had to run away."

And there Mort says it, out loud: Jack's fear that, at heart, he's a coward. That he doesn't truly want to help other people, that he runs from conflict and the emotions that come with it. He wants to be brave. In spiriting Pansy away, he thought he had been. But at what cost?

Pansy is slumped to one side, motionless. None of Mort's shouting has disturbed her, or more accurately, her Sight. Mort stares as if just now noticing her. He touches her shoulder but gets no response.

Mort swears again. "Oh, buddy. What happened?"

"The Sight, you asshole." Jack punches Mort's shoulder, not hard, but the outrage building in his chest needs an outlet. "It attacked five minutes after you left because you wanted more information about the hot spot."

"She's been out this whole time?"

"This whole effing time."

"Oh, Pansy-Girl." With gentle fingers, Mort brushes strands of hair away from her forehead. Maybe he whispers, or maybe Jack merely senses it, but the words *I'm so sorry* float in the air.

"I—" Jack begins, swallows hard and then continues, "I can't bring her back."

"Of course you can. You always can."

But Jack is shaking his head. Every time he sucks in a breath, pain wraps around his ankle and radiates up his leg, suggesting that this is more than a sprain. If he's medevac'd from the field at this point during the capstone? He absolutely won't be walking at graduation.

"Okay. Let me figure this out." Mort bows his head, rubs his brow. "All right. I'll go talk to Carmen and Sandeep, send everyone out again, then we can use the command post—"

"I think my ankle's broken."

"*What?*"

"On the way down," Jack adds. "Carrying Pansy, and the weight and ..." He trails off, because what else can he say than that he screwed up, irrevocably.

Mort slumps back, defeat radiating from him. "Well, this has been a banner day so far."

"Does that mean you found the hot spot?"

Pansy's voice brings them both up short. Mort scrambles forward, and Jack winces as Pansy shifts her position.

"What happened?" She blinks, takes in her surroundings. Her voice loses that post-episode sleepiness. "Wait. You're hurt."

"I'm fine, sweet pea. Probably just a sprain."

"No, tell me. How long have I been out?" She glances around again and pushes to her elbows. "What's going on?"

"Nothing you need to worry about right now." Mort inches closer, his voice full of hope. "But tell us, what did you see? Anything?"

Pansy blinks again, her expression not so much dreamy as concentrated. Jack hates this part, maybe more than the incapacitation. Mort's quest for every last scrap of information, his desire to win, no matter the cost—it dominates everything.

"Florence."

Mort casts Jack a look, eyebrow raised. "Really? Botten was being straightforward?"

Pansy's shaking her head. "But it wasn't Italy."

"How would you know, Pansy-Girl?" Mort says. "You've never been." His voice is lighter now, full of humor rather than admonition.

"No, it wasn't overseas, because it looked like Minnesota, but it wasn't that, either. License plates. That's it!" She looks to him and then Mort. "They weren't European, they weren't from Minnesota. Not Washington." Her forehead scrunches, and Jack fears she'll slip under again. But her expression clears, and she declares, "Wisconsin."

"That's weird." Jack has never heard of Florence, Wisconsin. He doubts such a place even exists.

Mort's staring into the middle distance as if it's not strange at all. Then he rouses himself and says, "Let me get Jack to the command post, and then I'll double back for you."

"I feel fine." Pansy pushes to stand, and her arms tremble. "Give me a minute. I'm sure I can walk and—"

Mort points to her blood-soaked field shirt. "Too many effing evaluators running around, not to mention Botten. I'll bring you back a clean shirt from somewhere. Maybe one of mine."

"Oh, please, no." She holds her nose. "Not that."

Jack can't help but laugh, even though it jostles his ankle and the resulting zing up his leg brings a spate of tears to his eyes.

"A *clean* one," Mort says. "I promise."

MORT REMAINS silent during the slow trek up the hill until they reach the halfway point. Then, almost under his breath, he murmurs.

"Steeped in ambition, avarice, and malice."

"What?"

"The effing Enclave. You know what they've done?" Mort doesn't wait for a response. "They made the capstone exercise Florence, Wisconsin. Ever hear of it?"

"The town, or the—?"

"Fiasco, as my mom calls it. It was her last field mission. She retired after that." Mort pauses and readjusts his hold on Jack. "You know the back stairs, into the kitchen?"

Jack has spent enough time at Mort's house, a fancy, old-fashioned Victorian, complete with a sweeping front staircase and a hidden one that—back in the day—the servants used. It's the perfect spot for eavesdropping.

"My parents talked about it a lot, late at night, at the kitchen table. I was worried and wanted to know why my mom was so upset." Mort's expression mellows just a bit. "You know my mom, nothing bugs her." Mort pauses, contemplates the sky over Jack's shoulder.

Jack does know Mort's mom, and the fact that Mort's always been closer to her than his father.

"But she lost one of her best friends on that mission." Mort pulls in a breath. "Marigold Little."

"*What?*"

"Yeah, I know. I mean, sure, Rose has made plenty of enemies, but this is unnecessary. There's a ton of field missions and screw-ups to choose from. It's like someone ran their finger down the class list, saw Pansy's name, and decided to stick it to Rose."

In his mind's eye, Jack can see someone in the Enclave doing just that. Using Pansy to hurt Rose. His heart aches for them both. He's sensed that the ties that bound Rose to her sister were strained, but they'd never completely broken, not even now, with Marigold long gone.

"But you know what, buddy?" Mort's expression shifts. The fire is back in his eyes. He tugs Jack just a bit closer, and heat brews between them. "They don't expect us to know *anything* about this mission."

No, they don't. Florence, Wisconsin wasn't one of the field missions dissected during their classroom training. They've never stepped through the pitfalls, the mistakes, the bad decisions. Never role-played the different functions and responsibilities. Much to Jack's relief. He hates role-playing exercises.

"They think they've set up a no-win situation," Mort adds. "I mean, they always try to for the capstone, right?"

Yes, the classes before theirs warned them of that. It's not so much about completing the mission but how much you get right, how you react when everything goes to shit. Half a day in, and it seems like everything already has gone to shit. Unless?

"Are you saying—?" Jack ventures.

"I—we can win."

"Are you sure it's Florence, Wisconsin?"

Mort falters, some of the confidence fleeing his expression. "Maybe seventy-five percent? Do you think you could research it, work your intelligence magic on it?"

"I can see what's in the database."

"It won't be much."

True, but it gives Jack a place to start. "If your mom was on this mission, there's a good chance other parents were, or they heard about it. I can interview everyone. Even rumors will help. If it looks pretty certain, that will help us come up with a likely course of action."

"Spoken like a true intel analyst." Mort pauses, his gaze on the ravine below. "Don't say anything to Pansy, okay? About Marigold, I mean."

"I wouldn't hurt Pansy or Rose like that."

"I know you wouldn't." Mort turns that piercing, blue-eyed gaze toward Jack, his voice softening with promise. "And, hey, you know I didn't mean anything about anything."

Jack purses his lips, but nods.

"So we're good, right? Still on for our after-graduation trip?"

"Still on." Jack means it, mostly. Just as Mort never means the words he spews in anger, mostly. Jack wishes Pansy could come with them, but that isn't possible, or even something Mort wants.

"All right, then." Mort adjusts his hold once again, levering Jack's arm over his shoulder. "Let's go win this thing."

CHAPTER 8
PANSY

Joint Base Lewis-McChord, Washington
Friday, August 24

In one corner of the command post, Jack sits on a folding chair, his injured ankle propped on another. We've pooled our cold packs, and occasionally, one of us—me, Carmen, Mort, or Sandeep—switches them out.

We should probably remove his boot, but Jack's afraid he won't be able to get it back on. He insists it supports his ankle. We should probably medevac him, but not on the first day of the capstone. And Jack hasn't stopped working. One at a time, members of our team sit opposite him while he asks questions and scribbles notes.

The next time it's my turn to switch out the cold pack, I whisper, "You're my hero."

He rolls his eyes, but I can tell he's pleased.

Mort has me back on fissure duty. We're down a squad, detained by the cadre at the outpost. No one's been "arrested."

Not yet, anyway. But they can't complete any missions, either. Then again, neither can the two squads Charlie sent to attack them. The cadre have detained *them* as well, under the guise of "witnesses."

"Told you so," Jack says, his voice rough from pain, but he's teasing Mort.

Carmen snorts a laugh, Sandeep smirks. Mort just makes a face and sends the squad not guarding the hot spot back out to mend yet another fissure.

"Screamers," I call out as the squad leader ducks from the tent. "Virtual ones." Those are easy to detect. Over the last six summers, I—or maybe the Sight—have learned to anticipate the cadre and how they deploy those. Real Screamers? Not so much. "Possible ambush," I add.

She gives me a wave in thanks, and the canvas flaps whoosh closed behind her, the breeze bringing much-needed fresh air. Still, it loses the battle almost immediately. Body odor, a coppery hint of blood, and mustiness from the canvas tent are far too much for a puny puff of air.

Beneath all that are words unspoken. I can taste them, and my umbrella trembles against my spine as if she, too, senses it. I *know* something happened when the Sight attacked. When I ask, Jack just smiles and shakes his head as if it's no big deal. He made up a story about his ankle for the rest of our team, one that involved a Screamer ambush on the way back from the latrine. Since this has happened to all of us—really, it's like the Screamers enjoy embarrassing us—no one questions this account. But I'm the real reason his ankle might be broken. I want him to at least be angry about that.

"It's okay, Pansy-Girl," Mort says when I try to talk to him. He squeezes my shoulder, then turns me toward the map once again. "It's fine. Do your thing and don't worry about it."

In the aftermath, I can discern what most likely did happen. There's a smear of mud and blood on the map. Tiny, but it's there, marring the hot spot. Beneath my feet? A few round holes in the tent's dirt floor, the sort only an umbrella tip can make. Holes that weren't there before the Sight attacked.

Someone—a cadre member, or worse, an evaluator—discovered the command post abandoned. Even finding the hot spot first won't compensate for that.

And that's all on me. I knew the Sight was hovering; I knew I should have locked it down. While the Sight is all about self-preservation, it's idiosyncratic and erratic. True, no one other than Mort and Jack can know about my Sight. Apparently, that's still the case. But in its quest to protect me, it may have ruined everything.

Worry churns in my stomach, tightens my chest. I'm not concerned about the Sight attacking again. It's so sluggish that I can barely grasp the location of all the fissures. If anything, it's a bit put out that I'm asking it to help so soon after an attack.

Mort has retreated to the corner where Jack is sitting, their heads bowed over the notes Jack's been taking. Mort looks so animated, so purposeful, and so hopeful that his mood is contagious. Carmen hums a pop song, and Sandeep sways side to side with the beat while updating his portion of the map.

"No," Mort says, his voice full of team lead authority. "I think we need to go for it. Mission at all costs."

That should probably be the official Enclave motto. Even though it's not, it's one Mort has embraced.

"Not this time, buddy."

The warmth in Jack's voice makes me shut my eyes against a sudden spate of tears. That earlier tension between them—a brewing unease that threatened to explode—has faded. They're friends again, maybe more than friends. My umbrella shudders with relief, and the movement loosens the strap. If you squint, you'd swear she's waving at Jack's umbrella. She flutters her ruffles just so everyone here gets the message.

She is incorrigible.

From the other side of the tent, Carmen laughs.

"This whole exercise is designed to play to your weaknesses," Jack continues. "Yours and Charlie's. No one's missed the fact that you're both risk-takers."

In the space between them, the accusation of *reckless* floats. Knowing Mort, he takes that as a compliment.

"So, are you saying we don't go in and lock down the hot spot?" Mort is shaking his head. "How can we possibly win—"

"We let Charlie do it."

"*What?*" Mort's outrage echoes against the canvas walls.

"We pull our squad back to a defensive position." Jack pauses, almost as if he sees those invisible threads that tie us all together. "No, first we swap out the squads. Move the fresh squad in and have *them* set up a defensive position around the hot spot."

"What on earth for?"

"Because it's not an ordinary level five hot spot. We don't want to lose anyone."

"Waste of time. No one here is at risk of the thrall."

"But in real life? If this were an actual mission, any one of them could be. We found the hot spot way sooner than they expected. If we keep that squad in place, they're all at risk."

"It's going to be big," I add. I don't need the Sight for that. It's there on the map, beneath that smear of blood, an unintentional portent. "It's going to open up, and it's going to be a mess to clean up. It's that kind of mission, the sort of mission where the Enclave loses people."

Mort and Jack stare at me. It's almost as if Jack winces at what I've said. But he turns his gaze back toward Mort.

"No-win, remember?" Jack says. "Wouldn't the Enclave throw the worst case scenario at us? You know they can tag any one of us as injured or pull us from the field at any time. Hell, they already have by tying up our squad at the outpost."

"Update on that?" Mort calls out to Carmen.

She shakes her head. "Still detained." She draws little air quotes around *detained*.

"Just because we've never *lost* anyone to a hot spot on an exercise before." And here, Jack draws his own air quotes. "Doesn't mean it can't, or won't, happen."

Mort grimaces. The cautious approach goes against everything he is. Carmen has locked eyes with Jack and is nodding in agreement.

"Yeah, I can see it," she says. "It's exactly what they'd do to you *and* Charlie. Look." She holds up the operations tablet. "We already have reports that the site is unstable and could, under the right conditions, open a portal. I mean, you could reasonably ignore all that. I bet that's what the Enclave did on the actual mission. I say we cede ground, let Charlie set up his squad, and then wait."

"And Charlie will rush in," Sandeep adds. He throws me a look, his dark eyes glinting with humor. "Right?"

"Yes, he will." I sigh. I hate to betray Charlie, but I'm Team Connolly all the way. Besides, everyone here already knows his weaknesses. "That's Charlie."

"Traitor," Mort mutters, but a grin is starting to bloom. "Okay. Let's figure this out."

They huddle, Mort, Jack, Sandeep, and Carmen, pulling together a plan, going over Jack's notes and all the information downloaded from the squads' umbrellas. For a moment, I consider the four of them. I am the odd one out, the only one here not destined for a field assignment. My heart thumps with a longing so sharp, my vision blurs. I turn toward the map and dash away another spate of sudden—and unwelcome—tears.

My umbrella flutters her ruffles in an attempt to cheer me up. I all but ignore her. I let my fingers travel the map, seek out fissures for our squad's next mission, and let teardrops hit the dirt floor beneath my feet.

"HEY, Pansy. Bring yourself and your umbrella over here."

My umbrella quakes with so much force, I'm propelled across the tent. I've dried my tears and made peace—once again—with my lot. My umbrella is so joyous, you'd think we're heading to a dance party rather than a mission briefing.

They make space for me in the huddle, and Jack holds out his hands. It takes me a moment, but I realize that he wants my umbrella, and she nearly tears herself from her cross-body sling.

"What's going on?" I ask, and unsling her. Oh, she's incorrigible, all puffed up with excitement and greeting Jack's umbrella as if they've been separated by years and miles rather than a few minutes and barely eight feet.

"We're going to set up a relay," Mort says. "Or, rather, Jack and Sandeep are, between your umbrella and Jack's."

"We can do that?" If so, that's news to me. The cadre have intentionally limited our ability to communicate. We have the tablets, one for intelligence and one for operations. We have the data our umbrellas collect, but the transfer is manual, essentially like plugging into a USB port.

What we don't have is an automatic relay, or the internet, or cell phones. A worst case, worst conditions scenario, because a hot spot can wipe out everything, including field agents. We need to know how to react in dire circumstances.

"My brother showed me how to hack into the relay and turn it back on." Here, Sandeep shrugs. "Said it might come in handy for the capstone. He learned how on his last field mission, from Henry Darnelle."

Mort grunts and gives his head a dismissive shake.

"What?" Sandeep says. "Principal field agent before twenty-five? Not too shabby."

"Actually, it's the shit," Carmen corrects. "That's what it is."

Mort rolls his eyes. "Nepo baby."

We all stare at Mort in utter incomprehension.

Carmen punches his shoulder. "My dude, this is the Enclave. Have you suddenly forgotten *your* last name?"

Arthur Connolly is the chair of the High Council, and yes, he and Mort are related. Although untangling the various branches of the Enclave's family trees is an exercise in futility.

"There's nepotism, and then there's *ne ... po ... tism.*" Mort draws out the word for all it's worth. "Darnelle senior sits on the High Council."

Again, we all go with a stare, because so does Mort's father.

"Fine. Doesn't matter. Henry Darnelle can kiss my ass for all I care. Let's just do this."

"What are we doing, exactly?" I ask. Considering the way my umbrella is frolicking, it must be something huge.

Mort graces me with a wide grin, his blue eyes dazzling despite the olive drab that surrounds us. "You, Pansy-Girl, are going out on patrol."

Oh. Yes.

It's huge.

CHAPTER 9
HENRY

Joint Base Lewis-McChord, Washington
Friday, August 24

The Exercise Simulation Center hummed around Henry, although the initial excitement had died down. This lull was expected after the first hours of the capstone. The center was set up in one of the hastily built World War II barracks that had yet to crumble or be torn down. Floors rickety beneath their boots, the whitewash nearly transparent with age. It was better than being out in the elements, but not by much.

Not that Henry minded being out in the elements. Sometimes, he preferred it. Certainly, he preferred it to being stuck at headquarters with all the Enclave's machinations.

The windows let in a surprising amount of light, and through one, a glimpse of Mount Rainier. From time to time, Henry found himself wandering to that particular window and contemplating the view. Something about it—its majesty, its permanence—

reminded him that all of this, his career, this life, was fleeting. Mount Rainier would remain long after he was gone. There was something deeply comforting about that.

Across the way, near the exercise map, Botten was congratulating himself on creating a no-win situation for this exercise. Florence, Wisconsin. Something about it pinged in the back of Henry's mind. At the time, he'd been too young and too preoccupied to pay much attention to the fallout, too busy graduating high school and prepping for his final year at the Academy. His father, however, had been aghast, called the entire mission a fiasco.

The Enclave had lost two of their best agents on that mission, one a relative, Gordon Darnelle. His father's grief had been tangible and deep. Henry remembered that, but little else.

Losing an agent was a worst-case scenario, beyond losing an entire task force. To Botten's credit, it did make an ideal framework for a capstone exercise. Henry pulled out his tablet and started searching.

Beyond the rudimentary details, his tablet yielded nothing. When he tried the Enclave's main servers, an *access denied* message flashed across the screen.

"Wouldn't want you giving away any secrets now, my boy."

Henry swallowed the curse forming on his lips. Leave it to Botten to monitor everyone and everything within his grasp. He clapped Henry on the shoulder, and it took everything in Henry's power not to flinch.

Instead, he met the older man's gaze and replied mildly, "Merely curious."

"Of course you are. I believe it's a family trait." Botten's words were equally mild, but beneath them, Henry discerned the dig. Whether Botten meant his father's side of the family or his mother's, Henry couldn't say.

The professor turned his attention toward the map that took up an entire wall. The cadre were busy brewing up new virtual Screamer attacks to supplement the real ones. This late in the summer, most of the actual fissures had been repaired and the Screamers themselves unduly chastised. Hardly a challenge for sixth-year cadets.

"Things are going quite well," Botten added. "I'm pleased. The exercise seems to be testing both Cadet Connolly's and Cadet Pulchenko's mettle."

It would continue to, especially if the squad guarding the hot spot remained in place.

"Have you given any thought to your next assignment, my boy?" There, beneath the innocuous question, a promise lingered. Although when Botten promised anything, it always came with a price and a complicated set of attached strings.

Somewhere far away. That single and undeniably lovely thought filled Henry's mind. Somewhere, if not beyond the Enclave's grasp, at least at the edge of its fingertips.

"Still thinking on it," Henry said.

"Well, don't think too long. All the good assignments will be snapped up."

By good, Botten meant soft. The Paris assignments, the ones in London and Venice. The ones where you never pulled on field gear and made sure your bootlaces were double knotted. Those weren't on Henry's agenda. As much as he loved his suits—and his fondness for a well-tailored three-piece suit ran deep—he loved the field more.

"I'll risk it." Henry was about to say more when his phone pinged.

Botten raised an eyebrow. "I'll let you get that." The professor turned, heading toward the exercise map and cluster of cadre, then paused. "Tell Agent Worthington-Wells I look forward to seeing her back in R&D in the not too-distant future."

What the ... how did ...?

Botten didn't elaborate.

Henry tugged his phone from his pocket. Yes. Gwyneth had sent a text. A single word.

Talk?

Henry supposed he could, considering he had Botten's tacit permission to do so in the middle of the capstone. That voice inside his head echoed, a soft, seductive refrain.

Somewhere very far away.

Not that he needed the reminder.

"Gwyneth?" he said when she picked up. "Is everything okay?"

"Yes, of course, of course. It's just, you know, it's just ..."

No, he didn't know, and Gwyneth never sounded this flustered or giddy. Not even when the Enclave granted her this research sabbatical in London.

"No," he said, drawing out the word, "because you haven't told me."

Here, Gwyneth laughed. No, she *giggled*. Honestly, Henry couldn't recall the last time he'd heard her do that. She was what? Ten? Maybe twelve? The Christmas her father had set up an actual chemistry lab in the basement of the Worthington-Wells mansion?

"Henry, it's just everything. The future, plans, things like that, and I was wondering how you were feeling about it all."

Ah, there it was. The reason for this call. "You mean our betrothal?"

Her exhale was so forceful, he could almost feel it against his ear.

"Yes." The word was clipped. "That."

"The same as ever. I haven't changed my mind, if that's what you're asking."

They'd agreed that—at the right time—they'd petition for an annulment. True, so few were granted, and generally under extreme circumstances. But Henry had the backing of his father, who sat on the High Council. Then again, Gwyneth's mother occupied a seat as well.

Ah. That was it, then. The snag.

"Are you getting pushback?" he asked, although he couldn't imagine how that might make Gwyneth giggle. Something else was brewing.

"No, it's not that. What I mean is, now that you're a principal field agent, I thought you might be having second thoughts." Before he could ask why, she continued, "I thought you might want to continue to follow in your father's footsteps."

To do so would mean honoring their betrothal. That was a prerequisite for a seat on the High Council, Botten being the lone exception to that implicit rule.

"I don't want a seat on the High Council, Gwyneth. You know I never have. If for no other reason, I lack my father's skill set for that."

She snorted. "Hardly."

But it was true. Henry hadn't inherited his father's patience with incremental progress, his unbelievably high tolerance for other people's bullshit, his stamina, and his grace. No, his father was a cut above everyone else who sat on the High Council. He was certainly a cut above Henry himself.

"What's this about, really?" They'd grown up together, and he *knew* Gwyneth. She was playing three-dimensional chess, and perhaps having a bit of fun at his expense.

Some of that earlier giddiness infused her voice. "I almost

don't want to say it out loud. I'm afraid to jinx it, if you can believe that. But, Henry, I think I've found the one."

For one brief moment, regret washed through him. No, he didn't want Gwyneth or the betrothal. What he wanted was wrapped up in the softness, the tenderness of her voice. He wanted someone to be as giddy and breathless about him as Gwyneth was about this mysterious someone.

And he wanted to be just as breathless and giddy in return.

"That *is* something," he said. "Is it too soon for congratulations?"

"Perhaps, by a bit. But you don't mind?"

"How could I?"

"Then will you give me your blessing?"

"You don't need it, but yes, absolutely."

The silence that followed was warm with the nostalgia of this odd thing between them, a relationship that was, and at the same time wasn't. What a strange burden the Enclave placed on their children.

"You know I'll always care for you, Henry."

"And I, you."

He was about to ask more, to see if Gwyneth was ready to share a few details, when a shout came from the other side of the room.

Gwyneth laughed. "How goes the capstone?"

Henry scanned the brewing crisis. "Looks like it's heating up."

"I'll let you go, then."

And Gwyneth Worthington-Wells hung up without letting him say goodbye. But then, she never did.

Henry tucked away his phone, crossed the room, and joined the others at the map. Unlike the ones in the field, their map was fully electronic, each squad leader's and team lead's umbrellas relaying their current location, giving the cadre and evaluators a full, real-time picture of the exercise.

"Cadet Connolly just pulled his squad from the hot spot," one of the evaluators told him.

Not a moment too soon.

"Cadet Pulchenko's moving in."

"That won't end well," Henry observed.

The hot spot was rigged to disintegrate at the least opportune moment for whichever team held it. A virtual portal would open that might, depending on other factors, swallow an entire squad. The activation was automatic, set up long before either team sent out their first patrols. By deploying his squad so close, Cadet Pulchenko was rapidly approaching the trigger point.

"We might be able to wrap this up early," Henry said.

The evaluator next to him gave him a grin. "From your lips," she said, and pointed toward the map.

Henry was about to ask her name when Botten pushed his way through the crowd and stood in front of the map's display.

"*What?*" The venom in the professor's voice silenced all but a few whispers near the edges of the gathering. Then those too died when Botten turned and narrowed his gaze.

Botten let his headmaster glare canvass the assembled group of evaluators and cadre. "I feel confident that none of you would play favorites." The cold and precise way he delivered this proclamation denied his words.

As if Botten himself never played favorites with cadets throughout their six summers at the Academy. As if the Botten's Best List didn't exist. As if he hadn't already promised both Misha Pulchenko and Mortimer Connolly, Sr. that each man's son would win the capstone. How Botten might appease both was a mystery to Henry.

The professor stood before them now, color high in his cheekbones. An odd, almost desperate look flashed in the man's eyes before it settled into something else, something that resembled loathing.

For the life of him, Henry couldn't say why Botten turned and let that loathing settle on him.

CHAPTER 10
PANSY

Joint Base Lewis-McChord, Washington
Friday, August 24

Mind you, I've patrolled before. In fact, I patrol all the time in King's End. This past spring, my mother sent me out on my own with her radiant rose-red umbrella, in preparation for this last summer at the Academy. I find and mend fissures and fight off plenty of Screamer attacks. And the Screamers of King's End? Insidious, with an uncanny knack for making those attacks personal.

But this! A real field mission, or something made up to look like one. No wonder my umbrella is so excited. She still is, trembling while Jack and Sandeep establish the relay.

"This isn't normal," Sandeep is saying.

I lean close, trying to discern what he's doing, but all I sense is my umbrella and Jack's happily communing.

"This rapport," Sandeep clarifies. "It doesn't just happen this quickly. Not usually, anyway. My dad says that sometimes it doesn't happen at all."

His father works in the Enclave's technology section, and Sandeep knows what he's doing and saying when it comes to umbrellas.

"They're friends," I offer. Everyone stares at me like I've uttered nonsense. Well, everyone but Jack.

"They are." He bestows a grin on both me and our umbrellas. "And always will be."

"Whatever it is," Sandeep says, "it's going to come in handy when we reach the hot spot."

Maybe the others can't sense it. Maybe it has something to do with my Sight and Jack's ability with connections. I'm positive my umbrella is more than a mere extension of myself. She is her own entity. Over the last several weeks, I've come to respect that.

She gives her canopy an indignant shake as if to say, *Well, it's about time.*

We must leave both Jack and his umbrella behind. He can't make this trek, that much is clear. We can't risk leaving the command post empty again, either. Although neither Mort nor Jack mentions *that*. The others don't know. I dread what will happen if—when?—our team loses the capstone, and they find out.

But Jack and his umbrella are crucial to Mort's plan. My umbrella will relay data to Jack's. He'll work his intelligence magic on it and send it back to mine. We'll have real-time information without having to send a runner to the command post to transfer data.

"Before you go," Jack says to us, voice plaintive, "could you at least hand me an empty water bottle to piss in?"

Mort heaves a sigh and shakes his head like a disappointed

father. "Next thing you know, you'll want one of those expired MREs."

But he lugs a pack of water bottles across the tent and lets them thump to the ground next to Jack's folding chair. Then he hands Jack his secret stash of trail mix.

"You're key to this, buddy," Mort says. "We couldn't do this without you."

My umbrella is nothing but fluttering ruffles as we leave the command post.

MORT HAS me situated well away from the hot spot. I can see it, and I aim my umbrella toward it so she can collect data.

"Don't need you falling in, Pansy-Girl," he says, a solid hand on my shoulder as if to anchor me in place.

No, I don't suppose we do. The hot spot doesn't look like much, but then again, this is an exercise. None of us has ever seen an actual level five hot spot. Maybe they look this benign, and that's what makes them so dangerous. Still, something swirls in my belly and is sharp against my tongue. Not a premonition. Not déjà vu. I want to call it both, but that doesn't make any sense.

It might be nothing more than the Sight messing with me.

I lock it down and focus on relaying all the incoming data. Mort pulls the squad at the hot spot's edge. They come rushing past me, each one reaching out to slap my extended hand. They'll set up a position behind us, watching our backs for any stealth Screamer strikes.

Mort crouches next to me while the fresh squad takes up a defensive position. "Far enough, you think?" He hands me a hand-kerchief.

Oh, Jack would not like this. I don't mind, although I think maybe I should. The Sight has perked up since its attack. It's right there, hovering again. The precipice opens before me. The sense of falling is so strong, I pitch forward. Mort has to grasp my shoulders again.

"Whoa, there, Pansy-Girl."

"Back," I manage. "Pull them farther back."

He jumps up, casting a look of alarm at me before herding the squad farther back.

The gush of blood is aggressive. For one horrible moment, I'm convinced it won't stop. Like at that picnic with Daniel under the willow tree, when I absolutely bled so much it was (almost) a medical emergency.

The farther the squad retreats, the slower the blood flows. It finally stops when Mort lands at my side again.

"You okay?"

I nod. The crumpled handkerchief is soggy, the olive drab so dark that it looks ominous. Mort swears.

"Don't tell Jack?" He pulls the handkerchief from my hand and hastily buries it, shoving it beneath the soft earth.

When Carmen crashes next to us only seconds later, Mort and I exchange a relieved glance.

"Charlie's moving in," she whispers and then points. "You can see his squad on the ridgeline."

We watch as Charlie leads his squad toward the hot spot. While I can't see his face, I imagine the wide grin and look of astonishment at this good fortune. Charlie never questions this kind of luck. If he doesn't learn how, someday, that will get him killed.

I lock down the Sight—yet again—before it can show me any details. There's nothing more the Sight likes to play than: *How will your friends die?*

I never let it.

"He should at least be a little bit suspicious," Carmen says.

"Who? Charlie?" Mort shakes his head. "Never. He knows Daddy is always there to catch him."

Both Carmen and I turn our skeptical gazes toward Mort.

"What?" he says. "Trust me, my old man could give a rat's ass about my ranking at the Academy. I'm doing this all by myself."

Behind his back, I catch Carmen's raised eyebrow and answer with one of my own.

But, yes, Charlie is marching in like he owns the world, or at least the hot spot. And he does move straight in, bypassing our earlier positions to start the lockdown phase of the exercise, the part that should, in theory, have him winning the capstone.

"*Oh.*" The word leaves me with a solid breath, like someone jabbed me in the solar plexus with the tip of their umbrella. I sniff and wipe away a small drop of blood from beneath my nose. The *lockdown*. That's what triggers the level five hot spot and opens a portal.

As if on cue, our world erupts. How the cadre managed that, I can't say. The ground quakes beneath us. Debris—filled with pebbles and dirt, pine needles and branches—launches into the air and then rains down on us. Someone's popped smoke grenades. The acrid stench clogs my nose and mouth while red, blue, and green smoke billows everywhere in great bulbous clouds, blocking our view of the hot spot, Charlie, and his squad.

"Keep sending data." Mort's voice is loud against my ear, but I can barely hear him above the shouts and all the noise.

I do as he says, gripping my umbrella tight, helping her maintain the connection with Jack's. We'll need this information to secure the hot spot ourselves.

At last, the smoke dissipates. The air is still hazy. The back of my throat aches as if I've been screaming, and my mouth tastes like soot. Mort lumbers to his feet but stays low. He shields his eyes with his hand, then nudges both me and Carmen with the toe of his boot.

I squint. There, at the edge of the hot spot, stands Charlie.

He is completely alone.

CHAPTER II
HENRY

Joint Base Lewis-McChord, Washington
Friday, August 24

Henry watched with growing amusement while Team Connolly neatly side-stepped the portal and began the lockdown phase of the exercise, the *actual* lockdown phase. It was a careful, meticulous operation, and the entire team deserved points for that. Mortimer Connolly, after all, was not particularly cautious, ever.

Clearly, he was listening to his intelligence and operations analysts. A rare skill for a cadet with such a hot head. When Botten exploded with another outburst and more accusations of cheating, Henry added some additional points.

Then he switched off the tablet, slipped through the group of evaluators and cadre still crowded around the map, and calmly declared, "We told them, didn't we?"

The sudden silence in the Exercise Simulation Center was delightful, if dangerous. Yes, Botten's mood was sour. Yes, Henry was skating toward the edge of acceptability. A principal field agent—even a newly minted one—had certain privileges, it was true. But not that many. Yes, he was being an asshole, and yes, he'd pay for this. Henry found he didn't care.

"About Florence," he clarified. "We told them about Florence." And by *we*, Henry meant Botten and his ridiculous speech about rolling hills and tree-lined—and ostensibly Tuscan—roads.

Botten turned, composed now, full of authority that only a member of the High Council could wield. "Go on."

Granted, there were any number of missions in and around Florence, Italy that the Enclave could have chosen for the capstone. None of these soon-to-be apprentice agents was foolish enough to believe that for long. Well, Charlie Pulchenko, perhaps. But even that could be excused. After all, he *had* been following the standard operating procedure for locking down a level five hot spot, as had the actual agents in Florence, Wisconsin. This sort of subterfuge was typical for the capstone—one more way for the professor to berate the cadets during the after-action review.

Henry made a show of switching his tablet back on and scrolling through the list of cadets on Team Connolly. "Given Cadet Ling's sense for connections and the fact that Cadet Connolly's mother was present in Florence, Wisconsin, I believe accusations of cheating are premature, at best."

Gwyneth had sent him that piece of information during Botten's initial meltdown, an exchange that had, Henry hoped, gone unnoticed.

He stared at Botten over the top of his tablet and added, "Who's to say they didn't figure it out?"

"Interesting theory. Perhaps these cadets need more of a challenge." Botten paused, tipping his gaze toward the rafters as if drawing inspiration from there. "Perhaps we render this particular exercise null and void and start from scratch."

Conjuring up another capstone scenario, pulling the teams back in and conducting another mission brief? It would mean at least an extra week in the field, a week no one wanted or could spare. Many of these cadets were slated to start college—some belatedly—along with internships. Others needed to return to their permanent posts. The families, the High Council, everyone would question why graduation had been postponed.

No one would like the answer.

Groans erupted. A few cadre members swore. The evaluator he'd spoken with earlier pinched the bridge of her nose and winced. The muttering intensified, and Botten let the discontent brew. No one chimed in. Given Botten's current mood, Henry supposed no one would, one way or the other.

"You're effing toast, Darnelle," someone murmured, the threat laced with both malice and anticipation.

At this last, Henry turned and speared the agent in question with a glare. A brute of a man, the sort with more shoulder muscles than sense. "Let me know when and where," Henry said, accepting the challenge. "And I'll be there."

His umbrella perked up at this.

"Don't get too excited," he whispered. "He won't follow through. More's the pity."

Botten took in the discontent and his expression shifted, anger replaced by perverse glee. The professor's screw-up—and it was, it really was—had become Henry's liability. It was there in the man's crafty smile, the glint in his eyes, calculating and cold. The benevolent headmaster of the Academy was a persona Botten donned, a cloak that he wore often enough to lull the unsuspecting into a sense of security.

Henry had stopped being fooled long ago.

"Well, then." Botten rubbed his palms together, the gesture

strangely eager. "It seems *Principal* Field Agent Darnelle has volunteered to run the after-action review."

Someone snorted a laugh and then covered the noise with a cough.

Botten pierced Henry with a stare.

"You have an hour."

JACK

Joint Base Lewis-McChord, Washington
Friday, August 24

Jack understands his fate, his role in the Enclave, and it's this. Well, not *this*, exactly. He assumes his eventual job at headquarters won't require him to piss in a bottle. Then again? This is the Enclave, so you never know.

He laughs at the notion of a cubicle farm filled with analysts, each chained to their desk, someone pushing a cart through the aisles, passing out bottled water and expired MREs. It won't happen, but he senses that, some days, it might *feel* that way.

Even so? This real-time relay with Pansy's umbrella? Almost worth the ~~broken~~ sprained ankle. He doesn't need to be on site to see what's happening. The data tells the story. And that ungodly burst an hour ago? His heart nearly stopped with worry.

But their team is all present and accounted for. Pansy and her umbrella counted them all. Pansy continued to send data and direct her umbrella even before Jack could prompt her for more, or a different angle. All he had to do was crunch the incoming information and send it back out to her so Mort could supervise the lockdown and the cleanup.

Might they win this thing, even after his screw-up? Jack touches the edges of hope, not daring to linger there. But he can't help it. The hint of that promise rides through the open tent flaps along with the breeze.

Then the sound of approaching footfalls pulls Jack's attention from this daydream and the tablet's screen. "Keep up the relay," he whispers to his umbrella.

A second later, Principal Field Agent Henry Darnelle steps through the tent door.

Oh, no. That hint of hope shrivels, and anxiety tightens his chest. He's caught. They'll pull him from the capstone. The certainty—that he's the cadet who won't walk at graduation—assails him. He grabs his leg, trying to leverage it off the chair. The ensuing spike of pain steals his breath. Sweat breaks out along his forehead. His eyes water, and he blinks, blinks, blinks away the tears.

"Cadet Ling, I'm glad I—" Agent Darnelle halts, tilts his head, and takes in Jack, his elevated foot, and the command post at large.

Henry Darnelle is a principal field agent for a reason; several, Jack assumes. First and foremost are his observation skills. The command post is a mess. Jack, too, is obviously a mess. He can't even explain why. He hadn't expected anyone to find him here alone, but maybe he should have.

Agent Darnelle unslings a messenger bag from his shoulder, already rummaging through its contents.

"Cadet Ling, you're injured."

It isn't really a question, but Jack nods.

"Do you mind if I have a look?"

Without recourse, Jack shakes his head.

Agent Darnelle kneels next to the folding chair propping up Jack's foot. With care, he peels back the sides of the boot and probes. Jack inhales sharply through his nose.

"Do you mind if I cut away part of your sock? I'd rather not yank on it."

Somehow, through the wave of nausea, Jack forces out, "Go ahead."

Agent Darnelle pulls several items from his messenger bag. He snips a careful line down Jack's sock, somehow avoiding the worst of the injury. His exhale confirms Jack's worst fears.

"Broken?" he asks, the word thick in his throat.

"Perhaps. It needs an x-ray, certainly."

"Can it wait?" Jack tries to keep the pleading from his voice, but it's no use. "I can't miss too much of the capstone."

"I don't think that will be an issue."

Jack lets his gaze dart back to the tablet. The readings have evened out, no more spikes of frenetic activity. Plenty of mending to do, but the cleanup phase of the operation is already in progress.

"Your team has locked down and secured the hot spot," Agent Darnelle continues, "and Cadet Pulchenko's team is out of commission."

"Oh."

To Jack's surprise, Henry Darnelle laughs. "Yes, indeed. You might say it caught any number of us by surprise. Neither team was expected to find the hot spot until day three, at the earliest, never mind lock it down." He considers Jack, a long stare that from any other Enclave member might send his heart into overdrive.

But there's something steady about Agent Darnelle, solid and sure. Mort doesn't like him, but then the list of people Mort doesn't like is endless. Maybe it has to do with the old families and the inherent rivalry, growing up in Seattle and in the center of the Enclave.

Jack's family lives in Portland, Oregon. The state has always been Ling territory, from keeping Portland as secure as possible to forays along the Columbia River and into the Cascades. Jack loves it there, and part of him doesn't want to move to Seattle after his two years in the field.

"May I?" Agent Darnelle holds out his hand, gesturing for the tablet.

Jack cringes in dismay but passes him the device.

"Hm." A long, unnerving pause. "I see you've managed to set up a relay."

"I know we weren't supposed to—"

Agent Darnelle halts his words with a single raised eyebrow. "Not use all the tools at your disposal?"

"But—"

"The main reason the capacity is deactivated is, for the most part, you're all so new to your umbrellas. Establishing a rapport with another agent's is an advanced skill." Agent Darnelle scrolls through the readouts, the back and forth between umbrellas. "Which you seemed to have managed nicely."

"It was a team effort."

"As it should be." He passes Jack the tablet. But then Agent Darnelle sighs, considers Jack's wounded ankle and then the view through the tent flaps. "I'll be honest with you, Cadet Ling. I have a conundrum."

Something fizzles inside Jack, a tension that reaches its slender fingers, once again, around his throat. This time, they squeeze a fraction tighter.

"Several problems, actually," Agent Darnelle clarifies. "I need to commence the after-action review in"—a quick check of his watch—"about ten minutes."

"The AAR already?" Sure, they're clearly in the cleanup phase, but they're scheduled to stay in the field for an entire week.

"There's very little left for your team to do. In an actual scenario, you'd remain in place until the larger task force arrived."

That makes sense, but the capstone over? After less than a day? Jack is certain that's never happened before. Something about this unintended consequence feels precarious.

Agent Darnelle stares through the tent flaps again, his gaze on the middle distance. His thoughts are so sharp, so biting, that Jack feels them press against his chest. He doesn't need Pansy's Sight to know something is very, *very* wrong.

"We're in trouble, aren't we?" he whispers.

Agent Darnelle pulls his attention from the door and considers Jack. "I won't lie, Cadet Ling. Given how quickly your team found the level five hot spot, there have been accusations of cheating."

Now, Jack's heart flips in his chest. His palms are clammy, and he nearly loses his grip on the tablet. As it is, he clutches it tighter, as if that could help. Why didn't they think of this obvious outcome. They—really, Mort—were so hell bent on winning that *how* didn't matter.

As Jack knows all too well, the *how* matters, sometimes a lot.

"Can you explain how you uncovered the mission that the capstone was based on?" Agent Darnelle asks. "Because clearly you did."

How? What can Jack say without mentioning Pansy? How would they even know? Unless ...

Jack points to a notebook on the ground, one grimy with dirt, the pages filled with his scribblings. "Can you hand me that, Agent Darnelle?"

With the notebook in hand, Jack flips to the front. "Cadet Connolly was having me do research on all missions in Italy, even though we thought it was too obvious, but then you don't want to overlook the obvious, do you?"

"Not at all."

"Then I mentioned something about Florence, and that made Cadet Connolly think."

True, Mort isn't given to thoughtful contemplation. It was Pansy's uttering *Wisconsin* that triggered all this.

"His mother's last mission was Florence, Wisconsin." Jack presses his lips together, searching for the right turn of phrase. "I guess that made an impression at the time. So, he had me investigate that. There wasn't much in the database." He taps the tablet. "Probably on purpose."

"Yes, definitely on purpose."

"So I started interviewing all our team members, seeing what they knew, what they'd heard from their parents, even rumors." Jack turns the notebook so Henry can see the large, loopy scrawls, the name of a cadet at the top of each page. "From there, we figured out the best course of action."

It's as close to the truth as Jack dares, but he wonders if Henry Darnelle can sense the missing puzzle piece, that piece being Pansy. When he doesn't respond, Jack can't help but blurt.

"Was that cheating?" Because maybe it was. "On a real mission—"

"Wouldn't you use all the tools at your disposal? Look for patterns? Connect the dots?" Agent Darnelle sighs and contemplates the view through the tent flaps once again. "I'm inclined to say no, it wasn't cheating."

Jack releases an audible breath.

"But I'm a mere cog in the machine, if you will." His lips twitch. "Still, I've already pointed out to the cadre that if they hadn't wanted you to know, they shouldn't have waxed so poetically about Italy in general and Tuscany in particular."

By cadre, he absolutely means Botten. It's a sour, fetid aftertaste that lingers in the air, and it makes Jack's mouth taste even worse.

"But I need to leave for the after-action review, and if you're to complete the capstone, you need to be there as well."

Jack is shaking his head. He can't make the trek, not in time, not at all. Henry plucks a small container from the items he assembled earlier and unscrews the cap.

"This is special field issue." With the utmost care, he spreads the balm on Jack's ankle, on the worst of the bruising, the livid reds already turning purple at the edges.

The rush that follows has Jack leaning back in the folding chair and blowing out a sigh of relief. The pain fades, not to the point of vanishing, but enough where it's submerged. The injury still roils beneath the surface, but Jack can all but ignore it.

"You shouldn't walk on it." Agent Darnelle holds up the container before securing the lid. "And, fair warning, this will wear off in a few hours. It's meant to help agents power through in the field, under dire circumstances."

Well, this is pretty dire, Jack thinks. He's still no closer to the actual after-action review, still can't make it there on his own.

"I can help you to my Humvee and drive you to the edge of the assembly area."

Jack's gaze darts to the map. He guesstimates the distance from road to hot spot. That's a lot of walking. Jack nods but opens his mouth to protest.

Before he can utter a word, Agent Darnelle adds, "Don't you have a relay set up?"

Next to him, the canopy of his umbrella swells with pride. Pansy will come for him. Jack knows this with absolute certainty.

So he accepts the help down the long hill to the Humvee, marveling at the man's deceptive strength—really, Agent Darnelle leverages Jack into the passenger seat as if he weighs nothing at all. His ankle throbs, although the pain is muted. Still, it's enough that Jack fumbles with his seat belt, his fingers clumsy.

Before they pull onto the road, Agent Darnelle removes that little container from his messenger bag and hands it to Jack.

"Keep it," he says. "It could be a long after-action review."

Jack isn't certain, but did Henry Darnelle just wink at him?

CHAPTER 13
PANSY

Joint Base Lewis-McChord, Washington
Friday, August 24

My umbrella is a near explosion of ruffles. She flings herself from my grip and launches herself into the air. She lands several feet behind me, turning tip over handle until she smacks the earth with what can only be described as an ungainly bellyflop.

She gives me no choice. I spring up and dash into the brush, hoping Mort won't notice this latest shenanigan. I catch up, scoop her from the ground, and give her a good shake. Not that it does any good. She's still tugging me forward. Behind me, a shout rings out.

"Pansy, what the hell?"

Mortimer. Of course it is. I'm about to turn around, or try to, when movement in the trees catches my eye.

It's Jack, leveraging himself from trunk to branch to trunk again, his progress clumsy and slow and painful. The Sight decides to let me know just how much agony he's in. I wipe my nose on the sleeve of my field shirt, not caring how much blood I leave behind, and race forward.

"No, really," Mort calls out. "What the actual hell."

Then he must notice, too, because footfalls pound behind me. A moment later, Mort sprints past. His speed always surprises me. For someone so large, Mortimer Connolly can *run*. He already has Jack supported by the time I catch up, a shoulder leveraged under Jack's, bearing most of his weight.

"Take the other side, Pansy-Girl."

I sling my umbrella cross-body and slip beneath Jack's shoulder to support his other side. My umbrella is agitated, a full-on flurry of ruffles. Jack's umbrella is a bit more sedate, urging her to calm down.

It isn't working.

"What's going on?" The words come out breathless. I can barely keep up with Mort's long strides.

Jack winces, and I want to tell Mort to slow down, but instead, he speeds up.

"They're calling the exercise," Mort says.

"What? So soon?"

"Yeah. Looks that way."

As if in confirmation, a long, shrill whistle echoes in the air.

Mort swears. "And we all need to be in the assembly area, ASAP."

"You didn't walk all the way here?" I say to Jack. The thought alarms me. "Did you?"

He winces again. "Not exactly. I'll explain later."

By the time we reach the assembly area, everyone else is gathering. Our squad from the outpost filters in, dragged out and muddy. They're followed by two of Charlie's. Considering how muddy *they* are, I wonder what went down at the outpost.

The cadets who were virtually swallowed by the portal—essentially the rest of Charlie's team—are already seated on the ground. I catch Charlie's eye and he gives me a half-grin. Then he spies Jack and his brow crinkles in confusion and concern.

We inch forward, Jack trying not to limp. Everyone makes room for him, blocking his ankle from view and scrutiny. We don't need the cadre asking too many questions.

"If they decide to make us do a forced march back to the barracks?" Jack asks.

Panic flutters in my stomach. The cadre might. They *have*. Repeatedly.

"We'll figure something out," Mort says, voice gruff.

"We'll carry you, man," Sandeep adds. "You're an effing hero. We won this thing. I know we did, and it's all thanks to you." When neither Mort nor Jack responds, Sandeep adds, "It's a lock."

Honestly, I suspect Sandeep is the only one who does believe this. Granted, Jack's in pain, but his eyes have that look that says he's holding something back. I can always tell. Mort grimaces and rubs his face.

We all huddle together while several unnerving minutes tick by, a replay of this morning. Was it really this morning? Yes, it was, and now we're playing the Enclave waiting game once again. The cadre and evaluators are all here. But there's someone who isn't, and I suppose we can't start without him.

At last, a Humvee rumbles down the road. Professor Botten, still in pristine field gear, emerges. He walks toward us, long, slow claps punctuating each step. The sound is rancor itself. When he reaches the middle of the assembly area, he takes a measured turn, piercing as many of us as he can with his glower.

"Did it occur to any of you that your two teams were supposed to work together?"

Behind him, the cadre and evaluators exchange dubious glances.

Mortimer chokes back a dismissive snort. "Like that's ever happened."

"Did it occur to you that there are no teams on a field mission?" Professor Botten drones on despite the cadre's obvious discomfort and while the evaluators scroll through their tablets as if they've missed something crucial.

"They think we cheated," Jack whispers when Botten swings around to berate Charlie's team. They're sitting opposite us, and not even Charlie can muster a smile under the onslaught.

My breath stills in my throat. I think of what I've done: used the Sight to help Mort win the capstone. But what if that was absolutely the wrong thing to do? I can't imagine the Enclave failing half the class.

But they might.

The thought is insidious and sour. If there's a single surefire way for the Enclave to never discover my Sight, it's this:

Fail.

Have I done that? And brought Mort and Jack along with me?

At last, Professor Botten runs out of ire. He gestures to the group of evaluators, and one of them steps forward.

"And now, Principal Field Agent Darnelle will conduct the after-action review. Try to pay attention." Botten says this as if the after-action review will be far more stultifying than his previous lecture.

Mort moans like it most definitely will be. "Shit," he murmurs. "Wish I had some toothpicks to prop my eyelids open."

Jack leans forward. "I think it'll be good. He's interesting."

Mort rolls his eyes.

"Besides," Jack adds, "he's on our side."

"Hardly."

I burrow against Jack, careful not to bump his ankle. Agent Darnelle is giving us some sort of history lesson. I think? A minute in, and I've already lost the plot. He isn't boring. In fact, his speech, or rather his tone, is reassuring. But it's no match for the words playing in my head, the insistent nattering, that one single horrible thought.

We might fail.

And it's all my fault.

CHAPTER 14
HENRY

Joint Base Lewis-McChord, Washington
Friday, August 24

Henry waited on the back stairs of the Exercise Simulation Center. The Pacific Northwest sun was making a grand appearance through the clouds, casting its light on the evergreens and warming his cheeks. It was such a spectacle that he considered driving west and catching the sunset along Puget Sound.

But no, if this class of cadets had to spend the next seven days in the field, he'd do so as well. After much debate, the cadre had decided to send the teams farther out, into nearly inaccessible areas of Washington state, have them mend every last fissure they could find and fend off actual Screamers.

In truth? A far more practical and useful experience than the capstone exercise.

No matter what Botten thought.

The door behind him opened with a screech of protest. Henry turned, alert, ready, and—if he were honest—itching for this confrontation. Instead of the brute, the agent he'd been speaking with earlier stepped outside.

"He's not going to show," she said, and settled next to him on the concrete steps.

"I was afraid of that."

"He's already heading for the McChord Club."

Henry laughed. "Of course he is."

She held out her hand. "Anisha Patel."

He shook it. "Henry Darnelle."

"Yes." She cast him a look, her lips twisting in amusement. Her face was framed by short dark curls. Her equally dark eyes glinted with humor. "We all know that."

"I suppose I've made myself a bit infamous."

"You already were."

Yes, Henry supposed he was.

"Nice after-action review. I mean, I still can't believe you—"

"Pulled it out of my ass?"

"Made it actually interesting, but yes, that as well. Seriously, no one fell asleep. After two weeks in the field? That's no small thing."

The sun was heading toward that golden hour glow. Maybe he *should* head for Steilacoom, at the very least, especially now that the promised fight wasn't going to happen. There was nothing all that enticing about his sterile hotel room on base. Or he could drive north and spend a few hours with his father, but the Seattle gridlock would eat up most of his time.

"They medevac'd Cadet Ling," Anisha said.

Henry nodded. "Good. That ankle needs attention."

"He's on my list. I'm inclined to pass him."

He suspected there was an ulterior motive for this conversation, not that it hurt to hash things out, have a sounding board. "Do so."

"You sound sure."

"I am. He's the one who pulled all the threads together on Team Connolly, the reason they knew the capstone was based on Florence, Wisconsin and what actually happened there. He has skills the Enclave would be foolish to ignore."

Anisha released a sigh, one filled with genuine relief. "That makes me feel better. What about Cadet Little? Things ended so quickly, I never really had a chance to see her in action."

"Who?"

"Cadet Little? Pansy Little? You can't miss her. She's the one with that pink, polka-dotted umbrella, the one with all the ruffles."

Apparently, Henry *had* missed her. He tugged out his tablet and started scrolling.

"It's a good thing she's slated for a permanent post," Anisha added with a laugh. "I can't imagine her on a field mission with *that* umbrella. It's not exactly subtle."

Considering that Henry couldn't recall Pansy Little, an outrageous umbrella might not detract. After all, Ophelia's was sage green and sparkled with so much glitter that it practically generated its own sunlight. His sister managed field assignments just fine, except when the Sight interfered.

He found Cadet Little's entry on his tablet, blinked a couple of times trying to picture her and found he couldn't. He continued to review her stats, her contributions to the team, her skills running the obstacle courses. It was all very mediocre and unremarkable.

"Oh," he said at last. "She's the one who was on the other end of the relay Team Connolly set up." Henry shrugged. "Well, if she can manage that, certainly she can do an adequate job as a permanent post agent."

His umbrella nudged him just a bit, as if it had an opinion about something, as if it wanted him to take a second look. Henry ignored the prompting, because frankly, there simply wasn't anything extraordinary about Cadet Pansy Little.

Anisha scrolled through her own list of cadets. "As much as I hate to say it, I must give Cadet Connolly high marks. He didn't implode, or lose his shit, and I was expecting both."

Henry laughed. "Yes. If he can keep things in check, he'll eventually step into his father's position on the High Council. Let's hope he matures before then."

"Probably not the High Council, not if the rumors are true."

"Rumors?"

"Not interested in his betrothed, not in the least."

"Ah. I see." He sighed and shook his head. "I wish I understood this obsession of the Enclave's." The weight of his own betrothal had lifted since Gwyneth's call. Still, things weren't resolved. Things might never be resolved, especially if the High Council denied their petition for annulment. "It's such a burden," he added. "Although—"

Henry broke off. The dual bands on Anisha's left ring finger were glinting in the sunlight, and dazzled his eyes for a moment. His own single band of exquisitely crafted platinum was now dull with grime. He should have it professionally cleaned after this time in the field. The notion added additional weight, one more chore, one more burden to attend to. He'd started wearing it when he turned twenty-one, as was customary. Not required, not explicitly. Still, wearing your betrothal band signaled that you were serious about your career in the Enclave.

"It looks like you've managed to make it work," he said, hedging a bit. Not every arranged marriage was a happy one—far from it.

She held up her hand and let the bands catch the light, her expression soft, her smile full of that tenderness Henry had detected in Gwyneth's voice.

"We'd hated each other since we were five and he ruined my birthday party," Anisha said. "Although he still insists it was my fault. We were the team leads for our own capstone. Even if we'd known about the point deduction for sabotage, we wouldn't have cared." She laughed, the sound warm with nostalgia. "You can imagine *our* lecture during the after-action review." She nodded toward the barracks behind them, where Botten and a few ass-kissers were still stewing and grousing.

"No doubt it's the highlight of the capstone for him, but I'm guessing this story has a happy ending?"

"They sent us out on a field mission together, and the rest is pretty much like a bad rom-com." She nodded toward his own band. "And you?"

"Let's just say things are in flux."

"Aren't they always." Anisha stood, brushed off her cargo pants, and then slung her umbrella cross-body. "Well, Principal Field Agent things-are-in-flux Darnelle, can I buy you a drink?"

"What did you have in mind?"

"I was thinking the McChord Club."

Henry felt his lips twitch. "Were you, now?"

"Decent beer on tap, an adequate selection of scotch."

"My reputation precedes me."

"It certainly does," she said. "But we should hurry, because I also have a hundred bucks riding on the fact that you're going to win."

CHAPTER 15
PANSY

Joint Base Lewis-McChord, Washington
Thursday, August 30 (the night before graduation)

The thump, thump, thump of my heart is almost more than I can bear. My eyes sting, and I'm seconds away from crying. I do *not* want to cry in front of Charlie. Of course, since there's a good chance I'll never see him again, maybe it doesn't matter.

His own eyes go wide. True, his father sits on the High Council, but getting caught outside his barracks tonight of all nights? Charlie might be looking at a permanent post assignment of his own.

Maybe they'll give him mine.

With admirable stealth, he rolls beneath my bed. Only the barest creak of the floorboards gives him away. Those I could explain with my own steps, not that I've moved.

At the last moment, his hand shoots out and grabs his umbrella.

The someone outside my room knocks on the doorframe. I manage a squeak in response.

The sheet billows. Then a man steps inside my room. He's tall, full of the authority and agency of his footfalls. The casual khakis are pressed with a knife's edge crease, and the polo shirt sports a logo that suggests it cost more than my round-trip flight to Seattle. He wears a forest green umbrella slung cross-body, one that emanates so much power, my own umbrella has gone utterly still against my spine.

He glances around, taking in the lackluster furnishings, and exhales a huff of amusement.

"How is it," he says, his voice low and warm, a hint of wonder infusing its tone, "that this never changes?" He heads for my closet, switches on the bare bulb light, and then steps inside. He scans the small space, his head turning one way and then the other. "Be sure to add your name before you leave," he says to me.

I'm frozen in place, my stomach iced over in fear, and I can't tell if my heart is furiously beating or has stopped altogether, and I swear my umbrella whimpers. I can't even give him a numb nod. He steps from the closet, and I'm stunned by a blinding smile.

"I believe you have something of mine." He leans over, hands braced on his thighs, and peers beneath my bed. "Charlie, I know you're under there, son. I'm sorry to say it's a no-go." The man, who must be Charlie's father, Misha Pulchenko, glances back at me. "There's no negotiating with your mother, but then, there never was."

My gaze goes from the rose discarded on the floor to the dark expanse beneath my bed, and back again to Misha.

"Exactly," he says. "I suppose it was futile to even try."

From beneath my bed comes the muffled and somewhat petulant response, "I don't want to marry Leah."

"You might express *some* regret about not being able to marry Pansy."

"She knows that."

Charlie's father looks toward me again. I shrug.

"She seems unconvinced, and perhaps relieved." Misha sighs. "Come on, son. I'm only allowed to intervene so much. We have an extremely tight window. If you don't want your first assignment to be a shit one, I suggest you get your ass in gear."

Floorboards creak under Charlie's weight as he squirms from beneath the bed. He pops up, curls askew, expression glum.

"Sorry," he says to me.

"It was never going to work." I know my mother well enough for that.

Misha steps into the hallway, but it's only to grab something. He hands Charlie a paper grocery sack, one filled with bright neon bags of chips and cheesy popcorn.

"A snack run is a forgivable sin, especially on the night before graduation. I recommend you don't get caught on your way back to the barracks, but if you do, you have an out. However, you were never here, never spoke to Pansy, and if you mention me, I'll deny everything. Got it, son?"

Wide-eyed, Charlie nods.

"Good." Misha ruffles his son's curls. "Now, get out of here."

Charlie's footfalls retreat down the hallway and then fade. It's almost like he was never in my barracks room at all, except for the wilted rose and the man who's still standing in the room's center. He's an older, more polished version of Charlie, curls shorter, glossy and tamed, expression a bit careworn. But the same hint of mischief that lights Charlie's eyes now fill his.

"Rose Little's daughter." He regards me as if he's searching for her in my features the way I found Charlie in his. "Remarkable. Give your mother my best."

With that, Misha Pulchenko leaves. I hear him murmur something on the way out, perhaps to our barracks monitor. Then, nothing. She doesn't come to check on me. The building is quiet and still, as if everyone else has fallen into a fitful slumber or is at least pretending to sleep.

I walk over to my closet and peer inside. If I stand with my back flush against its wall, I can see a legacy of cadets where the low wattage lightbulb casts a yellow glow against the wood.

My mother started her career as a field agent, no doubt bunked in the barracks across the parade field. I won't find her here.

I search anyway, trace last names I recognize and first ones I don't. Some are carved, with a pocketknife, perhaps. Others are written with markers, ballpoint pens, even pencil. I step from the closet and rummage around in my duffel until I find my own set of markers. My umbrella nudges me, just the smallest of suggestions. So instead of practical black, I select the frivolous pink.

I'm afraid the ink won't be dark enough, strong enough. That the pink will fade into the wood, and no one will ever know I was here.

Instead, my name practically glows. *Pansy Little, class of ...* I write.

And because pink was her idea, I add a sketch of my umbrella.

CHAPTER 16
JACK

Joint Base Lewis-McChord, Washington
Friday, August 31

"If you think this is boring," Mort whispers in Jack's ear, "you should hear him at Thanksgiving."

Arthur Connolly has been speechifying for a good thirty minutes, although if you asked anyone present, they'd say it feels closer to thirty hours, maybe thirty years. The day is clear, the sun warm and lulling. The outdoor graduation ceremony is an Enclave tradition. Something everyone is regretting at the moment, Jack suspects, from cadets to cadre. The sun bakes his head. His ankle, in its cast, aches and itches. He can't even pretend to scratch the maddening sensation. A clean break, the doctor assured him, but it would delay his first field assignment by at least six weeks.

Mort smells like deodorant soap mixed with whiskey or scotch or whatever the hell he was drinking last night. His eyes are bloodshot, and he rubs his temples from time to time. Jack stopped at one questionable and overly sweet concoction in a red cup, but the party went on for hours.

On his other side, Pansy yawns, and yawns, and yawns.

She didn't sleep last night. This he knows, the occasional vibration in the air alerting him to her worry. He yearned to tell her not to fret, except Jack wasn't certain they'd all be here this morning, either.

He can taste the relief in the air. Or maybe it's simply his own. His fear—that one of their class wouldn't walk at graduation—hasn't come true. He'd been so sure, too, so anxious. But they're all present and accounted for, every last one.

On the stage, one of the members of the High Council clears his throat, a gentle sort of nudge that, nevertheless, does the job. Jack isn't sure who, although the culprit appears to be Harry Darnelle, Henry Darnelle's father. It's there in the man's benign expression, the hint of amusement in his eyes. The only person not pleased or relieved is Professor Botten.

Not only doesn't Jack care, he's glad Botten's put out. There's something wrong about that man, and the professor's glare glides from one person to the next in a way Jack can't read but knows is important. For all his skills with connections, sometimes they fail him.

You have the knack, Jackie, his uncle always says. *Just be patient.*

It's hard when threads are right in front of him, ones he can't read. He wants to force himself to try, at least, but all around him, umbrella canopies begin to flutter with anticipation. His attention goes to the stage where someone is handing members of the High Council stacks of diploma holders, leather bound in oxblood, embellished gold embossing. Empty, of course, as if the Enclave doesn't quite trust their newly minted apprentice field agents.

Actually, Jack knows they don't.

It doesn't matter, because all of them are graduating. When

Mort is called up first, as top-ranking cadet, a long list of honors after his name, Jack wishes he could stand and cheer.

Even with the cadets ahead of him, there's no time. His own walk to the stage will be agonizingly slow. Pansy readies his crutches. She follows him, not only to help, but because she'll be called right after he will.

It's only when they reach the stage that he notices her expression, a bit slack-jawed with shock, with eyes full of chagrin.

Then? He sees what she does.

The steps. An entire flight of them, impossibly steep, perilously rickety, with no room for his cumbersome cast, never mind his crutches. His worry comes crashing down, and it turns out he was right.

Jack *is* the cadet who won't be walking at graduation.

CHAPTER 17
PANSY

Joint Base Lewis-McChord, Washington
Friday, August 31

How could anyone forget about Jack's ankle? Somehow, we all did. The Sight's been low-key nattering in the back of my mind, and I've been locking it down but hard. With all the members of the High Council? All the families? Too many people with intimate knowledge of the Sight means I can't risk the barest sniff.

"Maybe if ..." I trail off. I can't manage our combined weight, Jack's crutches, and two frantic umbrellas while navigating the narrow flight of stairs. Oh, our umbrellas are so upset, mine in particular. She's beating my spine as if this is all my fault.

Maybe it is. The Sight *was* nattering for a reason. I suspect this is it.

Then a cheer goes up, loud and raucous, our entire class on their feet, hands in the air. Then there's Mort. With purposeful strides, he crosses the space between chairs and stage. His grin is wide and dazzling, those blue eyes filled with so much affection, my heart grows tight in my chest.

"No, he isn't," Jack begins. "He can't be."

But Mort absolutely *is*. He scoops up Jack, and I catch the crutches before they hit the ground. Then Mortimer Connolly carries Jack Ling across the stage to accept his diploma.

My umbrella is abuzz, and tears flirt with my eyes. I blink a few times, hear my own name called, and mount the stage as well.

No one notices me, unremarkable Pansy Little, slipping in behind Mort and Jack. Our class is still on their feet, still shrieking. In all the commotion, I accept my own diploma holder from Misha Pulchenko.

He gives me a wink and then hands me something that looks like an airline ticket. I shove it into a cargo pocket and hurry down the opposite steps.

There, at the base, I'm captured in a hug, Mort and Jack swallowing me up. Carmen comes next, before Sandeep crashes into us. Even Charlie piles on. Then it's our entire class, teams forgotten, who won and who lost the capstone no longer important (although Team Connolly did win, no question).

My heart thuds. I wish things could stay like this forever. All of us here, laughing through tears, hugging each other tight, making promises I know we can't keep.

But for the moment, the air is sweet, as if those promises are real. And for a moment, I feel as if I belong.

CHAPTER 18
HENRY

What pleased Henry most? That this class had defied the odds? Everyone had graduated, and that was never guaranteed. Or perhaps it was Jack Ling. Yes, leave it to Mortimer Connolly to showboat. But there was no denying that tenderness, that joy. His heart was glad for them, for the entire class, really, there in their group hug.

It was, Henry knew all too well, the last time many of them would be together. All too soon, bitterness would chase this moment of sweetness. It was fleeting and oh so precious.

His umbrella nudged him, a poke in the small of his back.

"No," he said under his breath. "I doubt they want company of any sort."

Maybe his umbrella was feeling nostalgic as well. But it was enough to witness this moment, basking in the glow of what was, in the magnificent colors of all those umbrellas, canopies shaking with relief and glee. For a second, Henry thought he caught sight of that pink one, ruffles fluttering fiercely. Then he blinked, and it was gone.

He felt the shadow at his shoulder before the man spoke, caught the undercurrent of ire before naming it. Why the competence of this class triggered Botten, Henry couldn't say.

"I suppose, in the end, they earned it," the professor said.

Indeed they had. If there was a fissure left anywhere in the state, never mind on Joint Base Lewis-McChord, it was hardly worth noting. The military command was pleased, that much Henry knew.

"They comported themselves admirably," Henry replied.

"Odd how some of our more *seasoned* agents haven't, at least not on this particular exercise." Botten's gaze lingered not so much on Henry's face, which was unmarred, but on his knuckles and the telltale bruises that still discolored the skin.

Oh. So, somebody had tattled. Of course they did, possibly the agent on the losing end of this particular fight. There were rules against such things, these duels between field agents. But then there were also *rules*. The unwritten ones, the ones you ignored at your own peril. One of those rules was not backing down when your honor was at stake.

"I'm sorry to say, my boy, that you were a bit too slow on the uptake," Botten continued, not sounding the least bit sorry. "But I don't have much left by way of assignments. You can always spend a few months at headquarters—"

"What do you have?"

Botten's grin was sly, a curving, almost sensuous thing. Henry nearly took a step back but stopped himself. You didn't cede ground to Botten, not if you could help it.

"Six months in the Falkland Islands, but—"

Henry choked back a laugh. He'd be pulling on field gear for *that* and making sure his bootlaces were double-knotted.

"... I have any number of special duties that—"

"I'll take it."

"Pardon?"

"I said, I'll take the assignment, the Falklands."

Botten raised an eyebrow, conducted a judgmental, and skeptical, survey of Henry's three-piece suit and the polished wingtips, and then shrugged. "If you're sure, my boy."

"Absolutely."

Henry hid the sigh, his smile, the lightness that filled his chest. Yes, he'd take it.

Somewhere very far away.

Indeed.

CHAPTER 19
PANSY

Seattle-Tacoma International Airport, Washington
Friday, August 31

Even though Mort jokes about shoving me from the car—and watching me tuck and roll through the departures lane—he pulls his Audi into the airport parking garage and we circle until he finds a spot. Once we have, he and Jack accompany me into the airport, where the crowds are already thinning since it's late in the day.

Yes, *graduation* day. It's like the Enclave can't wait to send me back to Minnesota and King's End.

Mort is gabbing about his first field assignment with his mentor, one that will send them to Cabo San Lucas. Yes, *that* Cabo San Lucas. This is not an assignment; it's a boondoggle. A frown clouds Jack's brow. He pushes alongside me on a knee scooter—one Mort got for him—the wheels whispering, his knuckles white on its grips.

"It might be different when you don't have Pansy there feeding you information," Jack mutters.

Mort scoffs as if he's never once asked me to use my Sight when Jack wasn't around.

"He'll be fine." This is one thing I know about Mort, without question. He'll always find a way to manage, always land on his feet.

It's Jack I worry about, not just his broken ankle, but all of him. As if he senses that worry, he turns his attention from Mort and gives me a brave smile.

"We'll visit," he says. "Every year."

This is, if not a lie, something that won't come true. But I nod, swallow back my tears, and smile in return. Even if I'm not destined for adventures, I'm certain Mort and Jack are.

We linger in the check-in area until I'm paranoid that security might round us up. I hug Jack, then Mort, and then Jack once again. I feel those threads between us, the strands woven over six long summers, strands so strong, they'll never break. But right now, it feels as though they're fraying at the edges.

"I have to go," I say. "And so do you."

They have a three-hour drive to Cannon Beach, where many of the old Enclave families have vacation homes. Mort has planned a whole trip, an entire week along the Oregon coast before they need to head back to Enclave headquarters for their first assignments.

As always, those of us with permanent posts simply go home.

I walk them to the elevator and try not to yelp when they vanish behind the closing doors. Then I lug my duffel bag and myself to the check-in counter, where I present both tickets to the representative.

"I have two," I say, apologetic.

She scans them quickly. "Oh, you've been upgraded to first class, that's all."

I have?

"You also have a club pass," she adds.

I do?

"You can head through security." She graces me with a smile, double-checks the tags on my duffel, and says absolutely nothing about the black, oblong case that secures my umbrella.

I pass through security as if I'm the most boring thing the agents have seen all day. With hesitation, I present the club pass, and I'm waved inside. Drinks and snacks are free, the chairs are leather and sleek, and I sink into one after loading up a plate with the sort of food I haven't seen in twelve long weeks.

I gaze out at Mount Rainier, the oblong case resting against one knee. I don't have a phone to stare at. I left mine at home, and soon, a new Enclave-issued one will arrive with my diploma.

Even though I've shut down all the electronics on my umbrella and she is in stealth mode, I sense her. She's determined and full of herself, as if we're headed to Cabo San Lucas rather than King's End.

The urge to tug her from her case nearly overwhelms me, but I do crack the lid and peer inside. Her ruffles flutter.

"Okay, we'll do this," I say, and then glance around to make sure no one is watching me talk to an inanimate object. "We'll do this together."

I only secure the lid when my flight is called, and then with reluctance. My heart is less battered. While I miss Mort and especially Jack, a warmth soothes the rough edges. I am not alone. When I sling my umbrella's carrying case over one shoulder, I know this:

We'll handle everything King's End might throw at us.

Together.

ABOUT THE AUTHOR

CHARITY TAHMASEB has slung corn on the cob for Green Giant and jumped out of airplanes (but not at the same time). She spent twelve years as a Girl Scout and six in the Army; that she wore a green uniform for both may not be a coincidence.

After twenty years as a technical writer, she now writes fiction full-time. Her short speculative fiction has appeared in *Flash Fiction Online*, *Pulp Literature, and Escape Pod*.

See what she's up to at https://writingwrongs.blog/

ALSO BY CHARITY TAHMASEB

THE CHRONICLES OF KING'S END

BOOK 1: *THE PANSY PARADOX*

BOOK 1.5: *THE CAPSTONE CONUNDRUM*

COFFEE & GHOSTS SERIES

AVAILABLE IN EBOOK, PRINT, AND AUDIO

Coffee and Ghosts, Season 1: Must Love Ghosts

Coffee and Ghosts, Season 2: The Ghost That Got Away

Coffee and Ghosts, Season 3: Nothing but the Ghosts

Coffee and Ghosts, Season 4: The Ghosts You Left Behind

YOUNG ADULT FICTION (WITH DARCY VANCE)

The Geek Girl's Guide to Cheerleading

Dating on the Dork Side

YOUNG ADULT FICTION

The Fine Art of Keeping Quiet

The Fine Art of Holding Your Breath

Now and Later: Eight Young Adult Short Stories

SHORT STORIES

Straying from the Path, Stories from the Sour Magic Series of Fairy Tales

Dragon Whispers: Six Tales of Dragon Adventure and Lore

Here's How We Survive: The (Love) Stories for 2020